The Adventures of Lettie Peppercorn

by Sam Gayton
and illustrated by Poly Bernatene

MARGARET K. McELDERRY BOOKS
New York London Toronto Sydney New Delhi

MARGARET K. McELDERRY BOOKS
An imprint of Simon & Schuster Children's Publishing Division
1230 Avenue of the Americas, New York, New York 10020
This book is a work of fiction. Any references to historical
events, real people, or real places are used fictitiously. Other
names, characters, places, and events are products of the author's
imagination, and any resemblance to actual events or places or
persons, living or dead, is entirely coincidental.
Text copyright © 2011 by Sam Gayton
Illustrations copyright © 2016 by Poly Bernatene
First published in Great Britain in 2011 by Anderson Press Ltd.
Published by arrangement with Anderson Press Ltd.
All rights reserved, including the right of reproduction in whole
or in part in any form.
MARGARET K. McELDERRY BOOKS is a trademark of
Simon & Schuster, Inc.
For information about special discounts for bulk purchases, please
contact Simon & Schuster Special Sales at 1-866-506-1949 or
business@simonandschuster.com.
The Simon & Schuster Speakers Bureau can bring authors to your
live event. For more information or to book an event, contact the
Simon & Schuster Speakers Bureau at 1-866-248-3049 or visit
our website at www.simonspeakers.com.
Book design by Deb Sfetsios-Conover and Irene Metaxatos
The text for this book is set in Adobe Caslon.
Manufactured in the United States of America
1215 FFG
2 4 6 8 10 9 7 5 3 1
CIP data is available from the Library of Congress.
ISBN 978-1-4814-4769-0 (hardcover)
ISBN 978-1-4814-4771-3 (eBook)

FIRST
EDITION

To Erin, who is Boss.

The Adventures of Lettie Peppercorn

PART ONE

In the Land of Albion

"Of bodies changed to other shapes I sing"

Ovid, *Metamorphoses*

❧ CONTENTS ❧

A RECIPE FOR SNOW:

A never-before-seen meteorological phenomenon

Made with LOVE, ALCHEMY, and the following
INGREDIENTS (listed in their order of use):

A length of silence, at least one hundred years long
Dust motes, charged with static
Seven drops of æther
Six dice
One teaspoon of salt
A string of frost, threaded through an icicle
A gray cloud, spun upon a silver wheel
Water

INSTRUCTIONS:

Cut the century-long silence into seven tiny moments.
Sprinkle the moments with dust and static.
Add a drop of aether to each.
Then throw in the dice (which ensures the snow
remembers to have six sides).
Repeat this six times (for luck).
Stir in a teaspoon of salt (so the snow will melt).
Sew everything inside the cloud, using the icicle needle
and thread of frost.
Finally, add water.

A Stranger Arrives

On a winter night so cold and dark the fires froze in their hearths, snow came to Albion. It came packed up in the suitcase of a stranger. Lettie was the first to see him.

The stranger walked up from the harbor, dragging his luggage *bump bump bump* over the cobbles of Barter town, searching for the sign of the White Horse Inn. He found it on Vinegar Street, swinging from the porch of a house on stilts. Up above, through the little kitchen window, Lettie the landlady watched him come.

With her telescope, she traced the long line of

s etched behind him in muddied frost. She put a hand on the ladder that led to the door and start to climb, up through the black and swirly night. The Wind was so strong it could have whisked away the fingers from his hands, and he wore no gloves. It was the coldest winter Lettie had ever known, and he was by far the coldest guest.

His teeth were blue.

His hair was white.

His fingers were blue.

The whites of his eyes were blue, and his pupils were white.

"A man with an icicle beard," she whispered to Periwinkle, who had just flown inside. "Where will we put him? All the beds are taken."

Periwinkle cocked his head and Lettie sighed. For a pigeon, he was a good listener, but he was terrible at conversation.

Lettie closed her telescope with a *snap* and dropped it in her apron pouch. She went into the tiny front room, where her two guests—a Lady from Laplönd and a Bohemian jeweler—sat in armchairs by the hearth. Their real names were signed in the guestbook, but Lettie called them the Walrus and the Goggler. The Lady was the Walrus, because she was fat with whiskers. The jeweler was the Goggler, because she did nothing but stare. They suited Lettie's names better than their own.

"Someone's coming up," said the tiny, shrunken Goggler. She hooked her scopical glasses around her ears and flicked down the lenses to glare at the door, her eyes big as saucers.

"He will *not* be having my bed," said the Walrus. Her wobbly lipstick pouted, her piggy eyes squinted, and her treble chins shook.

Lettie had no time to answer before the door flew open. On the porch stood the man with the icicle beard.

"I need a room," he said, "and it *must* be freezing!"

At once, the fire died down to embers. The Wind swept in, and before the Walrus could cover her ears, it snuffed out the ten tiny candles on her chandelier earrings.

"Yes," said the stranger softly. "This will do nicely."

His smile made a cracking sound, and a shard of his icicle beard fell to the floor.

Lettie stared. With jitters in her belly, she went to pick up his suitcase, but he shooed her with his hand.

"Get away," he said with a scowl. "Far too delicate."

"I'm not delicate," she answered. "I'm twelve."

"I was talking about my *merchandise*," he snapped, nodding at the mahogany suitcase. "It's very . . . sensitive. If it was spoiled, you wouldn't want to buy it. And I would have come all this way for nothing."

"Sir," said Lettie. "I don't know what you're selling, but I can't afford it."

"Don't be presumptuous," barked the stranger. "I know a customer when I see one."

The Walrus and the Goggler watched from underneath their furs.

Lettie was speechless. For a week she had heard nothing but:

"More sugar in the tea!"

"More blankets on the armchairs!"

"More wood on the fire!"

Now here was someone—a frozen man with a suitcase full of mystery—telling her that *she* was his *customer*.

Lettie Peppercorn, stop your gawping and say something, she thought.

"Welcome to the White Horse Inn, sir."

"Yes, yes!" he said impatiently. "Now fetch the landlord before I defrost!"

Lettie rolled her eyes. New guests *always* made this mistake. She wiped her hands on her apron. "*I'm* the landlady."

"You?" he sneered.

Lettie gave him one of her sterner looks. "That's right, sir. Me. Lettie Peppercorn."

"Well, what about Mr. Peppercorn?"

"Da's at the pub, if I had to take a guess. Down by the harbor, at the Clam Before the Storm, betting with the sailors."

The stranger pursed his blue lips in irritation. "And Mrs. Peppercorn?"

"Well," said Lettie hotly. "If I had to take a guess, I'd say that's none of your business."

"Girl, you have no idea about *my* business. Remember that. You're just a customer."

"I'm much more than that," said Lettie. "I wash sheets, I dust shelves, I tidy up rooms, and I brew a *very* good cup of tea."

"Her talents as a landlady," said the Walrus, "are satisfactory."

"But the decor is atrocious," said the Goggler, "and rather ugly on the eyes."

Lettie followed the stranger's gaze as it swept around the tiny room. The White Horse Inn was drab and bare. The pictures were gone from the walls, leaving dark squares on the wood. There was a dining table by the kitchen, two armchairs by the fire, and Ma's old pianola in the corner. There was one rug left. It was small.

"It looks cold enough," he said.

"But all our beds are full," said Lettie.

"I don't want a room for *sleeping*, girl. I want a room for *business*."

Lettie was in half a mind to give him a lecture on good manners and send him packing. But she couldn't. The White Horse Inn needed money. Da's gambling already had Mr. Sleech, the debt collector, knocking at the door each week. So instead of a telling-off, she gave the stranger a smile and showed him her wide, wonderful eyes: the eyes of her ma, long gone.

"Certainly then, sir. Bed or business, it's all the same rate here . . ." She stuck out her hand and said: "Three shillings a night, if you please."

"Three shillings is reasonable . . ." began the Goggler.

". . . for an inn with more than one rug," finished the Walrus.

"You can have any room you like for your business," said Lettie, ignoring them. Then she lowered her voice so the old ladies couldn't hear, and added: "Even theirs."

She expected him to haggle. He was a businessman,

and this was the town of Barter, after all. But he just scowled and said, "I better get everything I need from you."

"You will," Lettie promised. "With a brew and a smile."

"Very well," he said. "We have a deal."

Lettie had to stifle a cheer. She was so desperate for money that she would have taken two shillings. Three would cover all of Da's debts for tonight. If she sent them to him now, he wouldn't have to borrow from Mr. Sleech, the debt collector. And that meant that Mr. Sleech wouldn't come around at midnight for the last rug.

Three cheers for the man with no manners and an icicle beard! she cried out in her head.

Lettie realized that she didn't know his name. He hadn't introduced himself, which was strange indeed, especially since he was a businessman and she was supposed to be his customer. She wondered if it would be rude to ask, but before she could he bent down suddenly and picked three pebbles from the black ice around his boots.

"Here," he said. "Put out your hand."

Lettie folded her arms instead. "Sir, I asked for three shillings, not stones."

"And I said, 'Put out your hand.' So stop your pouting and do as I say, girl."

Reluctantly, Lettie obeyed. He dropped the pebbles into her palm: one, two, three. Reaching inside his coat, he brought out a glass vial shaped like a J. It was filled with thick, silver liquid. He twisted off the cork and put a drop on each of the pebbles.

And something happened.

Something extraordinary.

The pebbles began to fizz. They jumped in Lettie's palm like crickets.

"Keep them in your hand!" said the stranger.

Lettie clasped her hands together, and inside the pebbles bounced around. Then the air went *pop!* three times, and they fell still. A little wisp of smoke wriggled from between her fingers.

"Finished," said the stranger, corking the bottle.

Lettie opened her hands.

She couldn't help but gasp.

The old ladies in their armchairs just stared, open-mouthed.

"Now," the stranger said, "we can get down to business."

But Lettie couldn't. She was rigid with shock. In her palm the pebbles were gone, and in their place were three silver shillings.

"How did you do that?" she whispered.

He put the bottle away inside his coat. "An alchemist can make anything he wants."

Lettie clutched the coins up in her fist. That word: *alchemist*. She hadn't seen an alchemist for years. Now there was one at her inn, making money from rocks and carrying a suitcase full of mystery. . . .

The last alchemist to stay at the White Horse Inn had been Lettie's ma. But she was gone now. She'd left three things: a note, her coat, and a hole that had never been filled.

"It's a long time since we had an alchemist here at the White Horse Inn," Lettie said to him as he fiddled with the straps around his suitcase. "The last one vanished through the window."

"I shall be keeping the windows shut," he said without interest.

"Did you know this inn was made with alchemy, sir? It started life as rubbish, rubbish that got mixed up in a cauldron with special alchemicals, and it all got changed and ended up a house—"

"I've no time for chatter!" he said, his temper sparking. "You're to do as you're told, or I'll turn those shillings back into pebbles just as quick as I made them."

Lettie scowled. "There're rules for staying here," she said. "The ledger's over there, and you've got to sign it. Your name, where you're going, and what you're carrying."

He strode up to the book, leaving frostprints as he went, and took the quill in his hand.

"Do you see his teeth?" murmured the Walrus.

"Bright blue," said the Goggler, filling a pipe with mint leaf. "And do you see that suitcase?"

"Mahogany," the Walrus said. She shivered and her chandelier earrings twinkled. "How unusual."

"How *interesting*."

Lettie rushed into the kitchen and took the room keys from the hook by the stove. Periwinkle fluttered on his perch, a message from Da dangling on his foot:

Nearly won the last game! Might borrow a few more shillings. Don't worry; I've got a good feeling about this! Da xxx

Da always had a good feeling after a few bottles of beer.

Lettie put that thought out of her mind quickly, before more bad ones came.

"Borrowing a few shillings?" she murmured. "Not

this time, you're not!" She turned to Periwinkle. "I've got a message for you to fly back in a bit, Peri. But now I've got to settle in the new guest. He's got a temper. He's got blue teeth too. Let me find out his name for you."

She went back into the front room with the keys. The alchemist threw down the quill and picked up his suitcase without a word. Lettie peered at the ledger to catch his secrets. Her eyes went wide when she saw where he had signed: the red ink had run blue.

Lettie looked at the quill, then back at the page.

He hadn't signed his name at all.

It just said *Snow Merchant.*

Lettie wondered. A merchant was someone with something to sell.

But what was *snow?*

An Invention Called Snow

"What's snow?" asked Lettie.

"You're my customer," said the Snow Merchant. "You'll find out soon enough."

There was expectation in his voice, like sparks. Lettie could tell he was excited. She could tell he was *nervous*.

Nervous about what? she wondered.

The Snow Merchant swung his suitcase up onto the table. Its legs creaked with the weight.

"I've never seen a suitcase made of mahogany before," said Lettie. "And I see a lot of suitcases in this business."

"It's bolted and buckled with lead," said the Snow Merchant.

"Must be hard to carry!" said Lettie.

"It keeps what's *inside* weighed down," he answered.

Lettie frowned. She had been landlady to dozens of guests, and they always brought with them one thing: luggage. There had never been a suitcase like this before. The prizefighters from Bavolga brought their leather boxing gloves, in search of new opponents; the chess players from Yssa brought their black-and-white boards, looking for new moves; the perfumers from Parall brought empty boxes, to catch new smells in . . . Lettie even knew where the Walrus was going next with her luggage: back to Laplönd with the Goggler, to show off the new chandelier earrings, which the Goggler had made.

But what had the Snow Merchant brought with him? What was the mystery he wanted to sell to Lettie?

Suddenly the clock by the bar chimed ten, and the Snow Merchant jumped. "The coldest hour of the night will come soon!" he cried in panic.

Lettie tore her eyes from the suitcase. "Is that bad?" she asked.

"It means there's no time!"

"No time for what?" said the Walrus.

"For the creation!" he said. "For the creation of snow! I have to *make* it before I can *sell* it, and to *make* it, I need a room!"

Lettie jangled the keys. "Which would you like, sir?"

"No, no!" the Snow Merchant cried. "There's no time to choose!" He looked around. "This one right here will do!"

And before Lettie could stop him, he strode up to the hearth to do battle with the fire. It hissed and spat at him, as if the two were old enemies. The Snow Merchant regarded it contemptuously and then plunged a hand into his huge, black coat. He rifled away, searching for something. Lettie heard the rustle and clink of bottles as he went through each pocket.

"Here it is!" he cried, withdrawing a small, crooked vial with a pipette lid. He shook it in front of his eyes and watched the contents slosh inside the glass. To Lettie, it looked like liquid frost: bitter blue, cruel, and cold.

"Oh, yes," he said, his voice soft with menace. "You know this, don't you? It's æther, isn't it? And it shall be the death of you."

The ladies in their armchairs whimpered, and Lettie

quaked and backed away, but she realized that the Snow Merchant wasn't talking to any of them: he was talking to the fire. Feeling rather foolish, she looked again to the flames as they squirmed in the grate.

The Snow Merchant unscrewed the lid and Lettie's goose bumps rose. The æther leeched the warmth from the room.

"Quite hard to obtain," said the Snow Merchant. "And quite impossible to bottle, but nevertheless, I *am* a genius."

He squeezed the pipette and it sucked up a drop of æther.

He turned to Lettie. "You might want to light a lamp."

"Why?" she asked, trembling. "What does æther do?"

He laughed at her, at the fire. "Why, it's an alchemical, of course. It's what we alchemists use to *change* things. Every alchemical works a different change. Mammonia, for example, changes pebbles into shillings. Gastromajus, another of my potions, changes people into their last meal."

"And what does æther change?" said Lettie.

"Why, *temperature!*" said the Snow Merchant, squeezing a drop of æther onto the fire. It snuffed out the flames in an instant, plunging everything into

Kicking Out the Breezes

Lettie stood in the front room, feeling the inn sway on its stilts and wondering how this night could get any stranger. The Snow Merchant had just asked her to get rid of the breezes, but how? Why?

"This is an inn built on stilts," she said at last. "You can't escape the Wind up here."

"Maybe that's why your guests do nothing but moan," said the Snow Merchant, and he laughed at his own wit.

Lettie scowled in the dark. She loved the Wind, she envied it: it traveled the world; it went wherever it wanted, while she was stuck inside, held prisoner by her job and Ma's last message. She looked over to the note, hanging on the wall above the door. It didn't matter that it was dark: she knew it off by heart. Just forty-three words, but they ruled her life:

LETTIE—THESE THINGS YOU MUST REMEMBER:

1. I've gone away to save your life
2. Until I return, you are in danger
3. The danger is inside Albion
4. Don't set a foot upon Albion, for it can kill you
5. I love you, and I'm coming back

It was because of the note that Da had raised the house on stilts. Then he'd made Lettie promise on her life that she'd do everything the note asked. She had tried everything to convince him to let her leave the White Horse Inn. When she was nine, Lettie had even made herself a miniature pair of stilts, so she could walk into town without touching the ground at all. But Da had shaken his head, like always, and said it was too dangerous.

Lettie didn't know what the danger was. She had asked Da, but he didn't know either. When Lettie was little they had sat long into the night, trying to figure it out. But, like an impossible riddle, Ma's words led them around in circles. "Let's sleep on it," Da had said, when the hour got too late. "Maybe we'll crack it tomorrow."

Now, Da left Lettie to wonder about the note all on her own. "Trust your ma," was all he would say. "Remember your promise."

It was a hard promise to keep, day after day, high tide after low tide, guest after guest. At least in the winter it wasn't so bad. She had Periwinkle and the Wind to talk to. She had her telescope. But still, sometimes it made her so angry she could scream. Ma wrote a note, vanished out of the window, and that was that: all the mothering Lettie would ever get.

Lettie Peppercorn, clear your head of all this useless thinking.

And so she did. Lettie set to work, chasing out the breezes. She followed them with a tea towel, all the way back to the places where they had wriggled in, then plugged up the cracks with newspaper or Da's old socks.

"Be off with you," she told the Wind, stuffing hankies in the keyholes. "You're good for keeping me company, but you're bad for business."

The Wind wasn't happy. It tickled the Walrus's

feet and knocked over Da's half-empty cup of khave. When Lettie finally shut it out completely, it whirled around, rattled the windows, and tried to sneak down the chimney. She covered the hearth with newspaper. The Wind howled and the timber stilts groaned. The house lurched forward, and the ledger fell from the table.

"You stop that right now!" Lettie called up the fire-place, and the Wind went still and sullen.

The Snow Merchant raised both eyebrows, which made crackling sounds. "I've never seen a little girl shout down the Wind before. It never does what I say."

Lettie shrugged. "That's because you've got no manners. What do we do next?"

He scowled. "Now we let the cold come," he replied. "We let it settle deep. And you can fetch me a bucket of water from the well."

The well.

Lettie clenched up like a fist. She was going to have to tell the whole room about her promise. Her anger churned away. She hated to say it, especially to travelers who came and went whenever they pleased. It made her feel so horrible, angry and ashamed.

"I can't go outside," she muttered. "Not even to the Vinegar Street well. If I climb down that ladder, I might die."

When they looked at her in confusion, she just pointed to the note that Ma had left. There was a silence as they all read it by the moonlight. The Goggler's scopical glasses made flicking sounds as she adjusted the lenses.

"How preposterous," said the Walrus.

Lettie looked at the floor. *Lettie Peppercorn, don't you cry, or swear, or do anything moody.*

"My ma wrote it down, just before she vanished ten years ago," she told them.

"How droll," said the Goggler.

Lettie wondered what "droll" meant. Perhaps it was a mix between "dreadful" and "dull." If it was, then that just about summed it up.

The Snow Merchant didn't say anything. His eyes were like frozen lakes. Lettie couldn't fathom his gaze.

"I'll do it myself then," he said sourly.

Lettie nodded. "The bucket's on the porch."

He stamped out the door and down the ladder.

Lettie took her two-draw telescope from her apron pocket and went into the kitchen, away from the piggy eyes of the Walrus and the glare of the Goggler.

"I wouldn't have fetched it for him even if I could, Peri," she muttered. "He's the rudest guest I've ever had. And he's put frostprints all over the living room."

She went to the window, pulled open the telescope with a *snap*, and put it to her eye.

The moon was out. All down Vinegar Street the gas lamps had been lit, and Lettie could see the cobbles and a hunched man upon them, riding a horse that seemed to hang between his knees. She turned her gaze down the cobbled street and into Barter, a place of brine and blubber and beer. Drunken sailors shone under the lights as they danced and tripped and fought in the streets. She knew those roads off by heart, though she'd never stepped down any of them: Briney Bridge. Swill Street. Pickle Lane. She looked to them. Then farther, to the ships moored on the jetty. Then farther, to the emptiness.

She looked back to the Snow Merchant at the well. It had frozen already and the coldest months were yet to come. The Snow Merchant picked up a stone and tossed it down to break the ice, then hauled up a bucket of gray slush and water.

"It would have been so easy," Lettie murmured. "To step down and get that."

The Wind blew fierce around the inn. *Remember your promise*, it seemed to be saying.

"All right," she said out loud. "I will, I will."

So Lettie did what she had to do in the moments

when she felt tempted: she thought of all the things that needed doing before midnight, and bed.

Periwinkle cooed on the perch by the stove.

"Peri!" she said, relieved at the distraction. "I've got a message for Da."

Lettie scooped up her pigeon and took him to the window.

"You look a little better today," she said, even though Periwinkle didn't. Lettie felt it was important to keep her sick patient in high spirits. "Less gray. Maybe it's the carrot peel I'm feeding you. Do you think you can deliver some shillings to Da for me?"

Periwinkle puffed out his chest and Lettie laughed.

"Silly bird. You're heavy as a stone but you still fly for me." She slipped the three shillings into a tiny brown envelope and wrote:

To Da, here are some shillings. A man with an icicle beard made them for me. Please don't bet them all at once, and please don't come back to gamble any more of the furniture. We've only got one rug left. Lettie.

She had a think, and added:

And IF you win big tonight, we need wood, coal, a new

broom head, herbs, carrots, candles, wool, a needle set, khave, paper, pencils, and soap. Oh, and loo roll! I'm not having you use the table napkins anymore, you hear? x

It was quite a lot to fit on one piece of paper, but she managed it. Tying the note and the money to Periwinkle's leg, she opened the window.

"You know where to go, Peri! Same place as always!"

With a *coo*, he spread his wings and struggled off into the night. Lettie watched him go. She loved that bird like the sea loved to roar. Along with the Wind, he was Lettie's joint best friend. Neither of them could speak (not in a language of words, anyway), but it didn't matter. Lettie did most of the talking, and Periwinkle tried his best to be a good listener. But still, she yearned for a friend who could talk back. Keeping her promise to Da kept her safe, but it kept her lonely too.

The Snow Merchant was back on the ladder, with the bucket heavy and slopping. Lettie helped him carry it up the last few rungs. He didn't even say thank you.

"I should have sent the boy to do this," he said anxiously.

"What boy?" said Lettie.

"The boy who brought me to Albion on his boat," said the Snow Merchant. "He was mooring his ship on the jetty. I told him to come up here with my stirring spoon."

"Maybe he got lost?" Lettie suggested.

"Impossible," he said. "I told him to follow my frostprints."

Lettie took her telescope and followed the Snow Merchant's muddy, frozen steps back into town. "Is that him?" she asked suddenly, pointing to a distant shape.

"About time," the Snow Merchant said, stomping inside. "Direct him up here, please."

The boy approached the ladder. He wore a thick coat with the hood up. He looked at the creaking stilts and the inn on top of them.

Then he looked at Lettie and waved.

What she first noticed about him, long before the stalk on his shoulder, were his bright-green eyes.

One Boy Travels
a Very Long Way

"Is this the White Horse Inn?" the boy called.

"It is, sir," replied Lettie with a curtsy.

"I'm not a sir," he said. "Just a sailor."

"Oh," she said. "Should I call you 'Captain,' then?"

The boy laughed and shook his head.

"So you sailed the Snow Merchant here?" she asked doubtfully. The boy didn't look like he could lift a spoon, let alone steer a ship.

The boy just shrugged and smiled. "I did. But right now, I'm just carrying luggage."

He held up what was in his hand: a large wooden spoon.

Lettie didn't know what to do or say back. She felt awkward and guarded. She had never met the other girls and boys from Barter, the ones who spent their days on the beach, combing the shingle for shells to trade. Sometimes she watched them with her telescope as they fought and laughed, their plaited hair whipping about them like angry arms. Sometimes they'd spot her, up at her window.

They shouted, "Your ma was trouble!"

They shouted, "Your da's *still* trouble!"

They shouted, "Where're your friends?"

But this boy didn't do anything like that. He just blew into his hands and said, "I'm not captain, or sir, or anything. I'm just Noah."

And with that, he scurried up the ladder onto the porch. Now that he was closer to her lamp, Lettie could guess his age. He was nine or maybe ten. Younger than her!

"Well, I'm Lettie," she said. "And I'm the landlady. And I'm twelve."

Then she reached out and took the spoon from his hand, adding, "And *I* do the luggage-carrying around here."

"Thank you," said Noah.

Lettie smiled, and together they stamped their shoes on the porch and went inside.

Now that his hands were free, Noah unwound the long strip of cloth wrapped around his shoulder. "My stalk was bent backward walking up from the harbor. I was scared it might snap!"

When Lettie saw the green shoot growing from his shoulder, she knew Noah wasn't from Barter, or even from Albion.

"You're from the Fifth Continent!" exclaimed the Walrus, stroking her whiskers. "How interesting."

"How exotic," said the Goggler.

"Not really," said Noah.

Lettie didn't know much about the Fifth Continent. No one did. It was so newly discovered, it hadn't even been named yet. She had heard the stories, though: every girl and boy there had a seed planted in their shoulder when they were a newborn, and it grew as they did.

"You've come a long way," said Lettie.

"I like to travel," he said with a shrug, as if crossing the entire Occidental Ocean hadn't really bothered him. The leaves on his stalk rustled.

"Welcome to Albion."

"Oh, I've been to Albion lots of times. Crossing the Channel is what I do. And while I'm here, I sell my flowers down by the harbor."

"Then welcome to the White Horse Inn," said Lettie.

His stalk bloomed: an orange flower.

"You're late," said the Snow Merchant, putting drops of æther on the rug. "Give me my spoon. At once, at once!"

He snatched his spoon from Lettie and began to inspect it. Noah's orange petals wilted and fell to the floor. In their place he grew a thorn.

The Snow Merchant seemed not to notice, or care. "You will wait for me to conclude our business, and then take me away from this wretched place. Is that clear?"

He swept off before Noah could answer, carrying on with his unfathomable preparations. The old ladies sat in their armchairs, looking bored and furious. The Goggler struck her tinderbox and lit her pipe of mint leaf.

Suddenly the Snow Merchant leaped forward, reaching out with his pipette. He put a drop of æther in her pipe before the Goggler could even draw breath. The smoldering mint leaf went out. Lettie tasted the æther in the air again. It made her head swirl.

"What have you done to my pipe?" cried the Goggler.

"I can allow no heat at all when I conduct my alchemy. That is why I am here: in the coldest room, in the draftiest inn, on the world's windiest shore, in the depths of the deepest winter."

The clock chimed eleven.

"And now," he added, "the night is darkest."

"Show us this snow, then," said the Walrus.

"I must make it first," the Snow Merchant replied, walking to his mahogany suitcase.

The Suitcase Opens

The Snow Merchant undid the straps on his suitcase and flicked the catches.

"Stand well back!" he cried, his coat billowing about him, his eyes blue and electric.

He lifted the lid and out it soared.

The Walrus gasped.

The Goggler rubbed her glasses.

Lettie looked at the ceiling.

"Is that . . . ?" she said to him, her breath catching. "Is that snow?"

The Snow Merchant looked down his long, jagged nose at Lettie and laughed. "Is that *snow*?" he repeated mockingly. "Of course it's not snow. Haven't you ever seen a nimbostratus before?"

Lettie hadn't. Never in her life.

Above the armchairs and the pianola there was a cloud. It swirled around the ceiling like it was desperate to escape. But Lettie had done her job well, and there were no gaps for it to squeeze through. The Snow Merchant wafted it away from the windows with his spoon.

"Now you understand why I told you to plug all those drafty cracks," said Snow Merchant. "It's very good at escaping through those."

Lettie was speechless. She tried to move her mouth, but nothing came out. She tried to say *How?* She tried to say *What?*

"*Why*," she managed at last, "is there a . . . *nimbostratus* in my inn?"

"It's here because I let it out of my suitcase," said the Snow Merchant. "And I let it out of my suitcase so I can make snow for my customer: you."

"But I don't even know what snow *is*," said Lettie. She pointed to the cloud. "And I certainly don't want *that*."

"Of course you don't. It's just a nimbostratus. Just . . ." He searched for the right word. ". . . equipment."

"Are you an alchemist or a merchant?"

"I'm both," he said. "I sell what I make. And what I make is snow."

Lettie thought for a moment. "Alchemists use cauldrons, not clouds."

"Think of it as a giant pot." He sounded pleased with himself. "A giant pot full of snow. But before that pot can overflow, we must all be cold enough. *All* of us."

He showed them his vial of æther.

The Goggler's huge eyes narrowed.

"That," she said, "is what ruined my pipe."

"Drink one drop and your fingers turn blue. Two drops, and your feet freeze the ground. Three drops lets me work with snow. I've never taken four. That would be dangerous."

The Snow Merchant rubbed his temples with his hands. Then he tipped back his head and opened his mouth. Lettie shivered: she thought he was about to scream. He raised his hand and squeezed one, two, three drops of æther onto his tongue. His whole body tensed inside his coat; blue nails dug into white palms.

The drops were making him colder. Dirty frost formed around his boots, and icicles dripped from his nose. His eyes turned from light blue to electric blue to ultramarine.

"Let the cold come," he said through clenched teeth. "Let it settle deep."

"Are you all right, sir?" asked Lettie, biting her lip.

"Of course I'm not!" he snapped. "I don't enjoy the æther freezing my blood and shattering my bones, but I am the only one who can create snow. And to create it, I must be cold."

He raised his pipette at the guests. At Lettie.

"And so must you. Open your mouths, please."

"I will not," said the Goggler.

"You just did," said Lettie, not quite meaning to.

"Don't be facetious," she answered back.

"What's facetious?" whispered Noah.

"I think it's Bohemian for 'cheeky,'" murmured Lettie. "But I'm probably wrong."

"This is most unusual," said the Walrus.

"If you want to see snow," the Snow Merchant explained crisply, "I must first *make* snow, and for me to *make* snow, the conditions must be right. And presently, the heat from each of you is ruining everything. Now . . . just a drop. It's quite safe. Even if I emptied the whole bottle down your throat, you wouldn't *die*." He smiled icily. "You'd just never be warm again."

Lettie started to shiver and wondered what it would be like if she never stopped.

The Snow Merchant continued: "I myself must take æther in order to handle snow: three drops, twice a day. You'll feel a coldness, but in an hour or so that will leave. Just one drop . . ."

There was a silence as everyone considered the choice before them, though for Lettie it wasn't a choice at all. The mystery had got hold of her: What was snow? Why was she the customer? Where was this all going? She looked over to the Goggler and the Walrus and saw that the mystery had a hold on them too. Meeting an alchemist was a rare thing. Seeing alchemy with your own eyes was even rarer.

Click! Click! went the false teeth of the old ladies as they opened their mouths.

"Excellent," said the Snow Merchant, giving them a drop each.

Noah was next. Then Lettie, last in line. She stuck out her tongue like everyone else had done.

The Snow Merchant squeezed the pipette and the æther fell.

Lettie felt like a fire inside her had suddenly gone out. Numbness filled her mouth and spread down her neck. She shivered and stamped her feet but she could no longer feel her toes.

"Your lips are blue," the Walrus said.

"So is your mustache," said Lettie, and the Walrus frowned. "Noah, there's an icicle on your stalk! And, look, you've even got a little icicle beard!"

She tried to laugh but could only shiver. They huddled together under the nimbostratus, their breath coming in faint white plumes from their mouths, and they watched.

The Snow Merchant took the bucket of grimy water and threw it into the cloud, which swallowed up every drop, rumbling greedily as it did so. He wafted the cloud into the middle of the room until it was above the rug, and then held up his big wooden spoon. He let a few drops of æther fall upon the end and began to stir the cloud with great, slow, circular movements that became faster and faster until the cloud was swirling, and the Snow Merchant was whirling underneath, and Lettie's head was dizzy from the smell and the sound . . . and then, all of a sudden—

Out of the cloud there fell a something.

Four amazed pairs of eyes watched it fall: tiny and pure white, drifting onto the rug without a sound. The Snow Merchant stirred the cloud again and all at once there were hundreds—thousands—of tiny *somethings* tumbling from the cloud to the floor.

"Lady and lady," said the Snow Merchant in a

flourish. "Boy and girl. I present to you: snow."

Lettie couldn't move, couldn't breathe, couldn't do anything but watch the snow fall.

"What are they?" the Goggler asked. She crawled over to the snow on the rug. Her scopical glasses had all their lenses flicked down and her eyes were huge. "Are they diamonds? They are! They are!"

"More precious than diamonds," said the Snow Merchant, his voice sinking to a whisper. "Each one tiny . . . unique . . . a treasure to behold."

Lettie was amazed and angry and afraid. There was more wealth lying on her rug now than was in the whole of Barter. Riches that Lettie would never have, even if she was a landlady her whole life. He expected her to buy these diamonds, with nothing in her pocket?

The Goggler began to babble very fast, sometimes in Bohemian. Lettie could just make out the words: "I must have snow!" And: "With snow I will make the greatest jewelry the world has ever seen!"

"I will wear it!" announced the Walrus. "Jewelry studded with snow!"

It seemed they had both forgotten about the chandelier earrings. Here was something more incredible by far.

"I will be the greatest jeweler in all the world!"

"I will look magnificent! They will finally make me

a duchess! The most elegant duchess in all Laplönd!"

But the Snow Merchant shook his head. "You are not my customers."

The Walrus laughed. "But we are rich!"

The Snow Merchant shrugged. "Normally your riches would be of interest to me. But Lettie Peppercorn is the only customer here that I will sell to."

Lettie looked at all the snow diamonds, a gleaming pile on the rug, and wondered how that could possibly be.

"Name your price," insisted the Goggler.

"I don't have one. Not for you."

The Goggler held up her long, bony fingers. "Look!" she cried. "Forty-nine gold rings, all from continental weddings that were called off!"

The Snow Merchant didn't even glance at them. His blue eyes were fixed on Lettie, and only her.

And still the snow fell.

And *still* the snow fell.

"Look!" said the Walrus, pulling a little hysterically at her fat, hairy ears. "Chandelier earrings! Priceless crystal! You *can't* refuse."

"I can," said the Snow Merchant. He turned to Lettie: "Go on, girl. Take them."

Lettie gulped.

He gestured to the drift of snow on the floor. "A pile of tiny, perfect diamonds."

Lettie didn't move, scarcely believing what he was saying. Leaning toward her, he whispered, as if he were sharing a secret: "They're yours."

Lettie looked at the diamonds of snow on the floor, seeing in her mind's eye the future they promised: a future with no more debts, no more bailiffs, no more rude guests . . .

"But, sir," Lettie said, her voice small, "I've got nothing to pay you with."

"It's a gift," he said.

It sounded too good to be true. A miracle. Only—and this was the *only* thing—the Snow Merchant didn't look like an angel. He looked crafty and devious.

"Why are you doing this?" she asked.

"I told you," he said cryptically. "I know a customer when I see one."

He was hiding something, she was sure, but his eyes were frozen and Lettie could not see past the ice. *A fortune, in exchange for nothing?* Fumbling with her apron, she tried to make sense of it.

In the end, she gave up.

"All right, Mr. Merchant, I'll take your snow, thank you."

With a low bow, the Snow Merchant began wafting his snow cloud back into the mahogany suitcase. He left the snow diamonds on the rug.

"It was a pleasure doing business with you," he said.

"It was hardly business at all," said Noah, mystified.

"Thank you," Lettie repeated, beaming her biggest smile. "Thank you!"

Realization was rushing through her: on the rug was a miracle, and it belonged to her. Now everything would be different. Better.

She suddenly noticed everyone was staring at *her*, waiting to see what would happen next. It was a strange sensation—Lettie was used to being told what to do. She felt a little awkward.

"What are you all looking at?" she demanded.

"You!" said Noah. "You're richer than an Albion princess, after all."

"Albion doesn't have a princess," said Lettie.

"It does now," said the Walrus bitterly.

Noah grinned. "How does it feel to be rich?"

Lettie thought for a moment. "It feels cold."

"Then we'll warm up!" said Noah. "Let's sweat this æther out of our systems, any way we can!"

"Warming up will be easy," said Lettie. "I brew a good cup of tea!"

She began to laugh. She laughed and laughed for the first time that day, and Noah laughed with her. Even the Snow Merchant joined in, although it sounded hollow. Like pennies rattling in a jar. He smiled but his eyes stayed cold.

The Walrus and the Goggler didn't smile, didn't laugh, didn't blink. The chandelier earrings seemed worthless now. They muttered to each other and they looked at the snow. They looked at the snow.

Lettie Peppercorn Brews Tea

Lettie went to the kitchen to make the brews. The Goggler and Noah followed her to the door. Noah was there to help. The Goggler was there to haggle.

"Three!" she cried.

"No, ma'am."

"Two then!"

"I said *no*."

"You won't miss two tiny handfuls of snow!" said the Goggler, her eyes as big as a puppy's.

"I'll haggle later," said Lettie. "I'm busy now."

The Goggler's eyes narrowed. "I'm trying to offer you a deal."

"Well, I'm trying to make the tea, and you're not helping." Lettie lit the stove and put the water on to boil. She sighed, feeling suddenly exhausted. "What is it you want?"

"One handful!" the Goggler declared. "My final offer!"

"I meant, what do you want in your tea?" said Lettie.

The Goggler scowled and muttered something in Bohemian. "Peppermint," she said. "And don't forget the rum." The inn wobbled a little on its stilts as she stamped all the way back to her armchair.

"Her temper could bring the whole house down," said Noah.

"And she didn't even say please," said Lettie with a scowl.

"Are you sure you want to leave her in there with all your snow?"

"Oh, forget about her, Noah. She can't do anything with the Snow Merchant still there. Let's make *tea*! That's what we need!"

Bounding over to the tea jar, she popped off the lid. It was empty. She showed it to Noah despairingly.

"Try this," he replied, and she looked on in amazement as fresh tea leaves unfurled from his stalk. He picked them and handed them to Lettie. "It'll kick the cold out of us."

Lettie looked at the leaves in her hands. "But that's *incredible!*" she said. "Noah, that's . . . well, it's just *stupendous!*"

"If you want more, just ask," Noah said. His flower blushed red, and he quickly turned away to hide the petals.

So they made tea, and Lettie gave her orders:

"Line up the mugs, please!"

"Turn on the stove!"

"Don't spill the milk!"

Noah did everything with a half-smile on his face, even when she told him off for letting his icicle beard drip into the cups.

"Do you *really* have to defrost everywhere?" she said, only half cross.

"You are too," Noah laughed.

"That's true." Lettie's nose was dripping, her bones were aching and she could *feel* the æther seeping out of her toes.

Just then Periwinkle came back through the window, the note and the shillings gone. Da had her message and his money.

"Bring Periwinkle down here would you, Noah? He needs his dinner."

Noah looked at Peri for a bit. Then he said, "This bird must be important to you, seeing as you can't leave the house."

Lettie stared at the water boiling in the pan, feeling a spike of shame. "How do you know that?"

Noah stroked Peri's feathers. "I read the note from your ma," he said simply.

There was a silence. Lettie searched for something to fill it with.

"Careful with Peri," she said suddenly. "Sometimes he pecks."

Noah picked him up, gasping. "And he weighs a ton."

"He does not!" Lettie flared.

"He does," said Noah, eyes bright. "Maybe you overfeed him."

"I feed him just right, thank you very much," she huffed.

"Only teasing," said Noah. "Sorry."

Lettie knew from his eyes and his smile that Noah had just been joking with her. But she wasn't good with jokes. She got angry and, before she knew it, she'd said something or thrown something that she shouldn't have.

"He's sick, if you must know," she said, trying to keep her temper. "Can't you tell?"

Reaching for Periwinkle, she put him by a dish of carrot peel, where he began to peck slowly at his dinner. "His beak is cracked, his feathers are gray, and he can't move his feet. Soon he'll be too heavy to fly."

She stirred the mugs and fished out Noah's leaves.

"What's wrong with him?" he asked gently.

"He's petrifying," said Lettie. "That means he's turning into stone. See how gray he is?"

Noah nodded. "Why?"

"Well," said Lettie. "My ma was an alchemist, and Da says that she made Periwinkle from a pebble she found on the beach. She plopped the pebble in her cauldron, threw in some alchemicals, and pulled out a pigeon."

Noah's eyes shone. "I thought that alchemists were just interested in selfish things, like making gold from lead. But making *life*? That's even more amazing than diamonds falling from a cloud."

"Well," said Lettie. "Now the alchemicals are wearing off."

"Just like the æther."

"That's right," said Lettie. "No alchemy works forever. You can change something but, sooner or later, the time comes when it changes back. And that's what's happening with Periwinkle." She turned to the pigeon. "Don't worry, Peri. Even if you turn back to stone you'll still be my joint best friend."

"Joint best friend?" said Noah, a smile on his lips. "Periwinkle and who?"

"You wouldn't believe me," said Lettie defensively. "My other friend isn't a person, either."

"Who is it then?" said Noah.

"The Wind."

Another child—a child from Barter—might have sniggered. But Noah had a plant growing out from his shoulder, so to him it didn't seem so strange that Lettie was friends with the Wind. He shrugged, then his eyes went wide.

"Lettie, you could pay an alchemist to cure Periwinkle!" he said suddenly. "Stop him turning back into a pebble, somehow. You could afford it; you're rich now."

"Maybe," said Lettie, and a tiny hope flared inside of her, like a flame. She felt a little warmer for a moment. "But . . . it's one of those laws of the universe, isn't it? Nothing stays the same. Things change."

She fell quiet and gazed out of the window, to the town huddled against the Wind. A place of brine and blubber and beer. A place she had promised Da never to go. There was mystery in that town. There were ships setting off for faraway places and others coming back with wonder and miracles . . . but Lettie wasn't allowed near them.

And now a miracle has finally come to me, she thought. *At long last, just when I needed it most.*

"The tea is ready," said Noah.

Lettie jolted from her daydreaming and turned around. The heat of the kitchen had changed him a little. With his coat off and his hood down, she felt like she saw him more clearly. She saw his goodness, his kindness and wisdom. And suddenly, she thought: *I want Noah to be my friend.* And Lettie wondered how she could make that happen, because she had never made friends with someone before.

Did she just ask? Is that what she had to do? She didn't want to just say it outright, for what if he said no, what then?

Lettie Peppercorn, you stop going red this instant.

"Well," she said, all of a sudden. "I'm Lettie Peppercorn and I'm very pleased to meet you."

Noah looked at her, puzzled. "I know," he said.

For a second, Lettie thought about boiling her head in the saucepan. It had all gone terribly wrong! But Noah smiled at her in his shy way, and she knew he understood.

"Lettie Peppercorn," he repeated. "I'm Noah, and I'm pleased to meet you too."

Lettie nodded, wiped her hands on her apron, and turned to the mugs.

"Well," she said. "I'm thirsty."

Lettie brought the mugs and Noah brought the spoons, and together they took them to the table. The room was dark and, it seemed to Lettie, full of secrets. No one had bothered to relight the fire. The Walrus and the Goggler were huddled, deep in whispers. The Snow Merchant stood by the rug, watching the snow glitter. It struck Lettie as strange that he was so fascinated by something he had just given away as if it were nothing.

Then Lettie lit the lamps, and the darkness fled, taking the secrets with it. The guests clustered around the steaming tea.

"This better be hot," sniffed the Goggler, big eyes blinking in search of her spoon.

"Have a sip and see," said Lettie.

She was expecting compliments, so she was very surprised when the old ladies started to scream.

"Outrageous!" shrieked the Walrus.

"*Scandalously* outrageous!" shrieked the Goggler.

"*Scandalously, OUTRAGEOUSLY AWFUL!*" shrieked the Walrus, not wanting to be outdone.

"Is it too hot?" asked Lettie, embarrassed.

In reply, the two ladies stood up and threw their spoons across the room.

"Not the tea!" gasped the Walrus. "The spoon! The spoon!"

She pointed. Lettie's eyes followed her finger.

Two brown sticks lay on the floorboards.

"Oh, yes," Lettie said at last. "That's been happening for a while."

"What sort of inn is this, where they give you sticks instead of spoons?" spat the Goggler, magnifying her scopical glasses to examine them.

"Calm down," said Lettie. "They're just sticks. You don't need to scream at them."

"But they *were* spoons," said Noah, blinking his green eyes at the stick he held. "I carried them from the kitchen. This one had a horse's head on the handle."

"Well, now it's just a stick. Don't worry, the same thing happened last autumn to all the knives."

"This is not the standard of service to which I am accustomed," said the Walrus. "I demand an apology! And an explanation! And a replacement spoon!"

"All we have left are forks," said Lettie. She sighed,

looking at the sticks and the tea splattered everywhere. It was going to be a nightmare to clean up, let alone explain.

"Then where is my apology and explanation?" the Walrus grumbled.

Lettie was too preoccupied with the spoons. She shook her head and frowned at them. "It doesn't usually happen like this," she said. "I wonder what it was that changed them back so quickly?"

"It was the boy," said the Snow Merchant suddenly, and everyone turned to look at him.

"Me?" said Noah.

The Snow Merchant chuckled. "You were carrying them, weren't you?"

"But I didn't do anything!" he protested.

Lettie suddenly realized. "Of course you didn't. It was your *stalk*."

"You've worked it out at last!" said the Snow Merchant. "The boy held them too close to his stalk, and all those *spoons* suddenly remembered they used to be *twigs*."

"So that's why it happened so suddenly," said Lettie. "I never knew that."

She thought of poor Periwinkle, and decided to keep him in the kitchen until she found a way to stop him perching on any slate roofs: he might petrify in an instant!

"I'm sorry I ruined your spoons, Lettie," said Noah, looking guilty.

"Don't be," said Lettie. "It just happens. My ma made these spoons, like she made the whole inn: she used alchemy. All that cutlery came out of a cauldron."

"I see," said the Walrus.

"It's quite a long story," sighed Lettie. "Years long in fact."

"At twelve o'clock, the æther will wear off and the room will no longer be cold," said the Snow Merchant, looking up at the clock hands as they twitched toward midnight.

"Tell us the story, Lettie," said Noah. "If it can make us forget the cold for ten minutes, it'll be a tale worth telling."

"All right," said Lettie, "as long as you listen and don't interrupt. Da told me this story. He used to tell it all the time. It'd be better if he was here, because he tells it perfectly. I can just remember the words."

Lettie began drawing up the story from her memory, like a bucket from a well. Da's words were hazy at first, but they became clearer and clearer, until she could almost hear him. It was the Da of long ago, the Da who used to sit by her bed and tell Lettie about her incredible ma; her incredible ma who was *coming back*, any day now.

Da never told stories anymore. And he had stopped saying that Ma was coming back.

Lettie Peppercorn, stop dithering and start talking.

"It all begins with a girl who just couldn't make up her mind," said Lettie. "Her name is Teresa. She's my ma."

The Making of the
White Horse Inn

*E*very Tuesday, Thursday, and Saturday, Teresa fell in
love. It was always with the same boy: the one who
lived on Gutter Street, mending nets for sixpence a day.
He had a bow tie and a stammer. On those three days
he came to her house every evening at six. He brought
flowers.

The boy and Teresa would go to the taverns, and
he would drink beer and she would drink apple juice,
right until the end of the night. Then they would search
Barter for a patch of stars among all the clouds to sit
under, and then the boy would ask, "C-c-can I kiss you?"
and Teresa would say, "Yes, Henry, but do it quickly,"

and then the boy would kiss her and say, "Can I m-m-marry you?" and Teresa would say, "Yes, Henry, but do it quickly," and then they would say good-bye and promise to meet tomorrow in whispers, because saying it too loudly might stop it from happening.

The other days of the week, she spent ignoring Henry Peppercorn.

"Put those flowers in a pot and go away," she said. "I've got work to do for Master Blüstav."

"But my d-d-darling—" began Henry.

"I'm not your darling," said Teresa. "I can't be Master Blüstav the alchemist's apprentice and your darling at the same time. There's just not enough days in the week."

"But the m-marriage—" began Henry.

"The marriage is off!" said Teresa. "I've changed my mind. I'm not going to be a wife; I'm going to be an alchemist."

Alchemists, Henry had realized over the past few months, were always changing things. Especially their minds.

"I'll be back tomorrow," he declared.

"It won't matter," said Teresa, shutting the door. "I've made my choice."

But come the next night, Teresa would be back under a patch of stars, head over heels in love with Henry

Peppercorn. That was the way it went; a day in love and a day out of love (apart from Sundays, of course, which they both spent in church, stealing furtive glances at each other while Reverend Gumpfrey droned on about the saints). On and on it went, for months and months. And if it had kept on going that way, Lettie Peppercorn would never have been born. But luckily for Lettie, Henry Peppercorn came up with a plan.

One Tuesday, as they walked arm in arm through the grim dark, trying to find a patch of stars to sit under, Teresa and Henry came upon a chessboard.

"How about a g-game?" Henry asked.

"This makes a change," said Teresa. "You usually ask if you can kiss me."

They sat down on either side of the chessboard.

"H-how about a bet?" Henry asked.

"What are we betting on?" asked Teresa.

"A question," said Henry, fighting his stammer. "And the question is: w-w-will you marry me? If I win, you have to answer once and for all, and then you can never change your m-mind again."

"And what if I win?" asked Teresa, who thought this outcome more likely, seeing as she was considerably luckier than Henry, and considerably smarter.

"Then I'll n-never ask again," said Henry with a

gulp. *"I'll l-l-leave . . . on a b-boat for B-Bohemia in the morning."*

"That would make my life much easier. I'd have my Tuesday, Thursday, and Saturday evenings free to study," said Teresa, although she sounded far from convinced.

And so they began. Teresa played black and Henry played white. It started badly for Henry. He never was much good at gambling (or chess), and before he knew it he was down to his king and two knights on horseback.

Then Teresa looked at her opponent in his bow tie, flowers wilting in his hand, and she realized that she didn't want to win, not if it meant never seeing her dear Henry again. And as she realized this, her pieces began to fall off the board, along with all her cares, and the more she began to lose, the lighter and happier she felt.

"Checkmate!" said Henry. "Will you marry me?"

"Yes, but do it quickly!" said Teresa, laughing.

They ran to the church on Steeple Street, woke Reverend Gumpfry, and were married at two in the morning.

As soon as the sun rose, Teresa went straight to Master Blüstav's laboratory, as usual. But when he tried to give her a lecture about alchemy, she just sighed and looked out the window. Then she showed him her ring and said:

"I can't be your apprentice anymore, Master. I'm Mrs. Peppercorn now. I quit!"

Blüstav, the Master Alchemist, was not happy. Teresa Peppercorn was his greatest ever pupil and, truth be told, she had more talent in her little finger than Blüstav had in his whole body. He might have his library, his laboratory, and his rows of neatly labeled alchemicals on shelves, but Teresa had imagination, which is by far the most important and useful thing for an alchemist to have.

Blüstav begged and pleaded for Teresa to stay. He admitted that he was a talentless old fool of an alchemist, that without her he couldn't even change a caterpillar into a butterfly. When that didn't work, he threatened and cursed. And finally, as she walked out the door, he promised her he would have his revenge.

But threats, curses, and promises of revenge had no effect on Teresa. She was in love. She dragged her small cauldron to the top of Vinegar Street, where she met Henry. He had just sold his house and net business for two shillings and sixpence.

"What shall I buy?" he asked, showing her the money.

"A place to put my cauldron," said Teresa. She looked down at the patch of stony ground beneath them. "Right here will do."

So Henry Peppercorn bought the patch of land at the top of Vinegar Street from old Mr. Pity, the woodsman. He had chopped down the trees years ago, and was just waiting for them to grow again, so he was happy to sell it.

The land was covered with rocks, pebbles, and boulders; twigs, sticks, and tree stumps; seaweed, shells, and a rusty anchor; silt, sand, and seagull poo; a broken chair, a chimney pot, and the skeleton of a horse.

"It's a d-d-dump!" grumbled Henry.

"It might be a dump, but it's got potential," said Teresa. And she began to work her alchemy.

In Teresa's cauldron, the rocks turned to armchairs, and the pebbles turned to plates. The boulders became four-poster beds; the twigs and sticks turned to beams and bricks that Henry arranged into bedrooms, hallways, and a kitchen. The seaweed turned to rugs with designs woven in the stitching. The shells made washbasins and a bath; the rusty anchor became the hearth; and the sand and silt became tiles that Henry nailed to the roof. There were a few things that stayed the same: the chimney pot stayed a chimney pot and went on top. The horse skeleton, they buried.

When they'd finished, Teresa looked up at the new house, and couldn't help but think that Master Blüstav would be very proud, and just a little jealous.

"That's why, every now and then, bits and bobs change back," Lettie explained. "In another few years, this place will be nothing but a pile of old rubbish again. No alchemy lasts forever."

"Ridiculous," said the Snow Merchant. "Ridiculous nonsense."

"It wasn't," said Noah. "It made the time go faster."

Lettie looked up. It was midnight. The ten minutes had flown by, as if the clock was eager to rub its long and short hands together for warmth. Just as the Snow Merchant had predicted, Lettie felt the last of the æther drain out of her. It left behind nothing but a dull, aching tiredness. She looked around and saw the last, faint shades of blue leave everyone's lips and faces. Except for the Snow Merchant, who was still frozen with æther. He had taken *three* drops, after all.

"It's good to be warm again," said Noah.

"I wouldn't know," said the Snow Merchant. His blue eyes were locked on the snow. He whispered something to himself, lips curling into a smile.

The Goggler spoke in Bohemian to the Walrus, and she nodded back.

Lettie looked at them both. Something wasn't right. She spotted what it was.

This time, it was her turn to point and yell. "You're *melting*!" she gasped at the Walrus.

"What?" snapped the Snow Merchant.

The Walrus put her hand to her head and screamed.

Something must have gone wrong with the æther, because from beneath the Walrus's wig, big drips were dribbling down her forehead.

"She's right, she's right!" cried the Goggler.

The Snow Merchant let out a yell of anger, and the old ladies shot from their chairs. The Walrus thrust a hand under her wig and brought out a handful of snow diamonds. Lettie's snow diamonds.

"Hey! They're *mine*!"

She had told the Goggler no, twice! But the old ladies had teamed up to take some snow anyway!

"Quiet!" barked the Goggler as she heaped a few snow diamonds on the tip of one finger and held them up to her eyes. She goggled for a long moment. There was a dreadful feeling in the air. Everyone looked furious, the Snow Merchant most of all: his teeth ground together and his face turned a deadly shade of blue.

"What's going on?" said Lettie. "Did you *steal* those?"

The Goggler yelled out in Bohemian, and whatever she was saying didn't sound very polite. She flicked away the snowflakes as if they were nothing, and even without scopical glasses Lettie could see why. The æther had worn off and the snowflakes were *melting*. They weren't diamonds at all, just water. Ordinary water.

Follow Those Frostprints!

"Swindler!" bellowed the Walrus, pulling off her powdered wig, tearing it in two, and throwing it into the fireplace. The handful of snow dribbled down her bald head, nothing but slush now.

"Charlatan!" growled the Goggler.

"I prefer the term 'fraudster,'" the Snow Merchant replied, edging toward the door and Lettie. "Out of my way, useless girl!"

But Lettie wasn't moving. She took her broom from its place by the door, and gave the whole room her sternest stare. "*Somebody* better explain what just happened. Before I start boxing *everybody* over the head with my broom."

"The diamonds melted!" said Noah, shaking his head in disbelief. "They're fake."

Lettie looked at the spreading puddle of water. It was true: she'd been made a fool of. Worse, she was back to having nothing.

It made her sick to her stomach.

"So I've been tricked, and I've been robbed," she said. "Who do I bash with my broom first?"

"*Them!*" said the Snow Merchant. "*They're* thieves!"

"*Him!*" said the Goggler and the Walrus together. "*He's* a liar!"

"*All of you!*" shouted Noah, and the inn went silent. "You old crones are despicable. Lettie needed those diamonds more than you ever will. She's got debts to pay, and new spoons to buy, and a hundred other things besides, and you stole snow just to wear it."

Lettie was speechless, just like everyone else. She had never had someone stick up for her before. Noah wasn't finished, either.

"And *you*," he said to the Snow Merchant. "You did the worst thing of all. You filled Lettie up with hope. You told her the snow was diamonds . . ." Noah trailed off and shook his head in disgust.

"Why trick me?" Lettie said to the Snow Merchant.

She understood the greedy old crones, but she could not fathom him.

"It was a test," the Snow Merchant spat. "And you failed. You were *useless*. I crossed oceans to find you, for nothing! I thought you were special. I thought *you* might . . ." He trailed off, looking bitterly at the snow. "I had predicted that this might happen."

"Really?" said the Goggler. "And did you predict *this*?"

With a mere flick of the wrist, she whipped a small silver pistol from under her skirt. She cocked it, ready to fire.

"What are you *doing*?" Lettie cried out in horror.

"Be quiet while I am aiming!" ordered the Goggler, squinting.

"I knew you two were horrible old bats! I never realized you were *murderers* too. Well, that's enough." Lettie held up her broom and waved the bristly end at the crones. "Get out! I'm—"

With a jerk, the pistol moved from the Snow Merchant and pointed straight at Lettie.

"You," said the Goggler, "are a very irritating girl."

"You can't kill me," Lettie said, clutching her broom. "I'm twelve!"

"I don't want to *kill* you," said the Goggler. "Not unless I have to."

"Then what do you want?" said Lettie.

"Isn't it obvious?" chuckled the Snow Merchant. "She wants the snow cloud."

"Of course I want it!" the Goggler ranted, her pistol whipping from Lettie back to the Snow Merchant. "It is incredible! It is *magnificent*! With those diamonds I could make jewelry fit for an Empress!"

"But they are fakes!" declared the Walrus. "Worse than Zirconium!"

"Only because they *melt*, you fritter-headed fool!" said the Goggler. "But we are on our way north, to a place even colder than here!"

"If we take the cloud to Laplönd . . . we can make snow that will never melt," said the Walrus slowly, as if just beginning to understand. "Not for a thousand years!"

"That is not how alchemy works," said the Snow Merchant. "You do not understand my problem."

"Oh, I am sure we could find a way," the Goggler mused. "We are rich. We can have anything we want . . ."

". . . and we want the snow cloud," the Walrus finished.

"But you can't *wear* snowflakes," Noah pointed out. "You could never make them into rings or necklaces; they'd melt in a moment."

"Not if I took a drop of æther every day," said the Walrus. "It would be a small price to pay for beauty."

Lettie shivered and wrinkled her nose. The Walrus was willing to be cold for the rest of her life, just to wear diamonds!

"You're mad, both of you!" she said.

The Walrus and the Goggler ignored her, staring wide-eyed at the Snow Merchant's suitcase, and Lettie saw the truth in her words. They *were* mad; they were obsessed. In their eyes was something Lettie saw in Da, every night before he went out gambling.

It was a kind of hunger, as if they had a hole in them that could never be filled.

Greed, thought Lettie. *It's got hold of them. Now they'll never stop wanting snow for themselves.*

"Give me the suitcase!" the Goggler said to the Snow Merchant.

"The æther too," added the Walrus, her chins quivering in excitement.

"I don't think I shall," said the Snow Merchant with a shrug.

"Then I will shoot you and take it anyway!"

There came a sound from the pistol, and though she had never seen a gun in her life, what Lettie knew in that split second was: *That is the sound of the bullet sliding into its chamber.*

Lettie's heart stuttered. Her legs quaked. She knew she had to take control of the situation and stop her guests from killing one another, but what could she do?

"What can you do?" gloated the Goggler. "You are trapped!"

"A situation I often find myself in," said the Snow Merchant calmly, tightening his white-knuckled grip around the suitcase. "Fraudsters like me become accustomed to making a swift getaway."

"Then I shall not give you the chance!" said the Goggler. *"Au revoir!"*

The Snow Merchant ducked.

But the Goggler was not aiming for him.

She pulled the trigger, and the silver pistol made a terrific *BANG!* that sent her flying backward and into the Walrus. The two of them tumbled head over heels into the armchairs, onto the floor, with the bullet thudding into the mahogany suitcase. It punched through the top and lodged itself in a lead buckle, an inch away from the Snow Merchant's heart. Instantly the nimbostratus began to pour out of the hole.

The Goggler might be mad, thought Lettie, *but she's clever too.* There was no way the Snow Merchant could make his escape now, with the nimbostratus leaking into the living room. He shrieked and plugged up the hole with his finger. The Goggler, in a heap on the floor, reached for her pistol where she had dropped it.

"Stop this right now!" said Lettie, springing forward. Moving on instinct, she took her broom and swept away the gun, sending it spinning under the pianola and into the cobwebs.

"No matter!" said the Goggler. "I always carry a spare!"

Pulling another silver pistol from her sock, she rolled off the Walrus, aiming for the mahogany suitcase again. Another bullet exploded from the silver chamber, thudding into the wood. A second hole! The Snow Merchant kicked off a shoe—which struck the Walrus on the nose—and jammed the hole with his big toe. With his free hand, he rummaged in his pocket.

"Stop fighting!" roared Lettie, but she could barely hear herself over her ringing ears. No one paid her any attention. The Snow Merchant and the crones were battling over the suitcase and the extraordinary snow that lay melting in a pile upon the floor. It was a fight that would be won by whoever was greediest, whoever wanted snow the most.

From his pocket, the Snow Merchant whipped out an alchemical bottle: a long, thin vial shaped like a J. The mammonia he had used to make the silver shillings. He uncorked it, to tip over the Walrus.

Lettie raised the broom again but it was too late. The Snow Merchant raised the mammonia—there was a blue flash and he yelped. The nimbostratus had thundered inside the suitcase and electrocuted him! He dropped the vial and Lettie batted it away with the broom, hoping to send it under the pianola or into the fireplace. Instead it flew through the air, hit the Goggler's pistol, and shattered.

The Goggler shrieked and began to jump and skitter across the room, just like the pebbles had done in Lettie's palm. Her hand and her pistol began to break up into tiny circles that Lettie realized were silver shillings. The fizzing stopped abruptly as loose change rolled all over the floorboards. The Goggler blinked three times at her missing hand, and fainted.

"I've got it!" cried the Walrus, pulling out the first pistol from behind the pianola. Her fat fingers couldn't pull the trigger, and Noah tried to wrestle it from her. She grabbed him by the stalk and screamed as his thorns cut her hand. In pain, she dropped the pistol, tripped over the Goggler, and stumbled toward the Snow Merchant, who reached for another vial. Not æther. Not the alchemical for shillings. Another.

With a laugh he shook a single pink-colored drop on the Walrus's bald, wrinkly head.

A hole appeared, billowing green smoke and sparks as it got wider and wider and filled with steam and tea. The Walrus screamed. Her skin turned to china. One of her ears grew huge and became a handle with a chandelier hanging from it; the other became a spout!

"He's turned her head into a pot of darjeeling!" cried Noah, and Lettie remembered the words of the Snow Merchant from before:

Every alchemical works a different change. Mammonia, for example, changes pebbles into shillings. Gastromajus, another of my potions, changes people into their last meal.

The Walrus's fingers felt around the edges of her head. With a trembling hand, she dipped a finger inside the steaming tea, and with a *thump* that set the whole house creaking on its stilts, she fainted too.

darkness and leaving a smell in the air, like the start of a storm. The ladies shrieked in their armchairs and the Snow Merchant cursed and cried out: "I told you to fetch a light!"

Lettie fumbled for the lamp in the kitchen and brought it out. After a while her eyes adjusted, and the Snow Merchant threw open the curtains to let in the cloudless night. In came the moonbeams. They pooled on the window ledges like wax. Everything now looked silver and expensive. The plates stacked by the pianola shone like shillings.

"I almost prefer it like this," Lettie said.

"I certainly *don't*," said the Walrus, rising up from her armchair, her mink coat wrapped around her. She wore a powdered wig one size too big, and it wobbled over her forehead. Her earrings tinkled and swung. "I am chilled to my bones!" she declared. "The least I deserve is a cup of *tea*! With cream and three sugars . . . make that five sugars."

"I will have peppermint," said the Goggler. "With a splash of rum."

But Lettie wasn't making tea. Her head was a kettle of questions.

"Do *you* know what snow is?" she asked the old ladies.

The Walrus smiled sweetly and said, "That is not the question you should be asking."

"Why?" said Lettie.

"And that is not the question, either," said the Walrus, in a higher voice.

"What's the question I should be asking, then?"

"The question," she shrieked, "is, *How many times does a guest need to ask for a cup of tea before she gets one?*"

"Be quiet!" said the Snow Merchant as he put drops of æther on the pianola keys. "You are lucky I am letting you watch my alchemy at all."

"Lucky?" cried the Walrus. "We are stuck on this drab little island, waiting for a ship that will take us to Laplönd! That is not *luck*, that is *torture!*"

The Goggler rubbed the rings on her hands. Lettie had tried a few times to count how many the jeweler wore. Almost fifty, she reckoned, and all of them were gold. A small fortune stacked on each long, bony finger. "I don't know what is worse," she declared. "The boredom or the frostbite."

"The Wind is worst of all," sniped the Walrus. "The inn sways so much I feel quite queasy—"

"I am trying to freeze this room!" thundered the Snow Merchant, slamming the pianola lid shut. "Yet you insist on filling it with hot air! *Sit down!*"

The Walrus looked at him, outraged. But she did flop back into her armchair.

"I want a cup of tea," she declared, waving a fat finger this way and that. "There should be tea and cake for a lady of *my* standing."

"Madam," said the Snow Merchant. "If you eat much more cake, then standing really will be an issue for you."

"How dare you? When we get to Laplönd, I shall be the height of fashion!"

"But for now, madam, you are just a blob of blubber, babbling nonsense," said the Snow Merchant. "So kindly shut up, and let me work."

Lettie clapped a hand to her mouth. *Lettie Peppercorn, don't you giggle.*

The Walrus sat numb with shock at being spoken to so rudely.

The Goggler stood to her full height of one and a half meters, and fiddled with her scopical glasses so she could glare at the Snow Merchant more ferociously.

"I am the most famous jeweler in all Bohemia!" she announced, in a voice full of accent and arrogance. "The Lady is my customer, and I demand you apologize at once!"

"Why?" asked the Snow Merchant simply.

"Because we are Ladies of Elegance!" spluttered the Goggler. "Because we are Women of Stature! Because—"

"I beg your pardon," the Snow Merchant interrupted, "but how can you be a woman of stature, when I mistook you earlier for a footstall? Sit down, you crinkled-up, craggy-faced crone!"

The two ladies seemed as lost for words as Lettie.

Finally, though, the Walrus recovered first from the Snow Merchant's astonishing attack of rudeness. Her chins were trembling with fury. "All I am asking for is a cup of tea!"

"My customer is too busy to make you tea," said the Snow Merchant.

"I am?" Lettie said. "I thought I was just standing here with my teeth chattering."

"Then do your job!" he snapped. It seemed even Lettie wasn't safe from his bitter temper.

"Job?" said Lettie. "What do you want me to do?"

"Get rid of the drafts, girl! Every last breeze."

t there on the spot, but nothing
;iddy with shock. Had the danger
lie?

Noah. "He's got a head start, and
those frostprints!"

wn Vinegar Street, following the
on the cobbles.

Lettie looked around her inn: the armchairs were broken, the rug was ruined, and the floorboards were soaked with tea. She dropped her broom, suddenly feeling very tired. Tidying up was going to take a long, long time.

"I didn't need your *meddling*," the Snow Merchant snarled.

Lettie gaped. "I wasn't meddling; I was trying to stop you from killing one another!"

"I could have beaten them without your help," he replied. "I don't need another apprentice."

"I'm not your apprentice," yelled Lettie. "I'm your landlady, and I'm evicting you! So get out!"

The Snow Merchant's face was cracked and black with fury. "Good riddance, girl. You're as troublesome as your mother!"

Those words to Lettie were louder than gunshots.

"What did you say?" she whispered.

Had she heard him right, above the ringing in her ears?

Of course she had.

"You knew Ma?" whispered Lettie.

"I did," said the Snow Merchant. "And now I must make my escape."

It was almost as if he had baited her on purpose. If

he had, it had worked: as he turned to the door, Lettie jerked forward like a fish on a hook.

"No, wait!" she cried, wishing she hadn't evicted him. "Stay!"

But the Snow Merchant had no intention of staying. He turned and threw himself from the porch. Lettie ran to the door and looked down, half thinking she would see him shattered upon the ground. But, somehow, the Snow Merchant had landed on his suitcase, and now he was hopping down Vinegar Street, unable to take his finger and toe from the holes, flashing blue with electric shocks. Then he must have plugged them with something, for he stopped hopping and broke into a run.

"He's heading to the harbor!" said Noah, stalk suddenly blooming a bright-red flower.

"He knew my ma!" said Lettie.

"He'll steal my boat!" said Noah.

Lettie looked back at the Walrus (her tea was draining out onto the rug and mixing with the slushy snow) and the Goggler (her hand vanished into a pile of shillings). She looked at Noah. He looked at her.

And together they said: "After him then!"

But as she surged forward, Lettie's eyes caught Ma's writing just above the door.

Lettie looked around her inn: the armchairs were broken, the rug was ruined, and the floorboards were soaked with tea. She dropped her broom, suddenly feeling very tired. Tidying up was going to take a long, long time.

"I didn't need your *meddling*," the Snow Merchant snarled.

Lettie gaped. "I wasn't meddling; I was trying to stop you from killing one another!"

"I could have beaten them without your help," he replied. "I don't need another apprentice."

"I'm not your apprentice," yelled Lettie. "I'm your landlady, and I'm evicting you! So get out!"

The Snow Merchant's face was cracked and black with fury. "Good riddance, girl. You're as troublesome as your mother!"

Those words to Lettie were louder than gunshots.

"What did you say?" she whispered.

Had she heard him right, above the ringing in her ears?

Of course she had.

"You knew Ma?" whispered Lettie.

"I did," said the Snow Merchant. "And now I must make my escape."

It was almost as if he had baited her on purpose. If

he had, it had worked: as he turned to the door, Lettie jerked forward like a fish on a hook.

"No, wait!" she cried, wishing she hadn't evicted him. "Stay!"

But the Snow Merchant had no intention of staying. He turned and threw himself from the porch. Lettie ran to the door and looked down, half thinking she would see him shattered upon the ground. But, somehow, the Snow Merchant had landed on his suitcase, and now he was hopping down Vinegar Street, unable to take his finger and toe from the holes, flashing blue with electric shocks. Then he must have plugged them with something, for he stopped hopping and broke into a run.

"He's heading to the harbor!" said Noah, stalk suddenly blooming a bright-red flower.

"He knew my ma!" said Lettie.

"He'll steal my boat!" said Noah.

Lettie looked back at the Walrus (her tea was draining out onto the rug and mixing with the slushy snow) and the Goggler (her hand vanished into a pile of shillings). She looked at Noah. He looked at her.

And together they said: "After him then!"

But as she surged forward, Lettie's eyes caught Ma's writing just above the door.

Don't set a foot upon Albion, for it can kill you.

"I can't go, Noah. The note."

"You don't have a choice, Lettie!"

"I won't break my promise!" she said fiercely. "It's the only thing holding me and Ma together."

"You've *got* to, Lettie. You've just got to! Don't stay because of some old note that's been nailed to the door for years. The Snow Merchant might lead you to your ma; he's what matters!"

Noah was right. If Lettie stayed, she'd never know the mystery of her ma's vanishing. For years now, all Lettie had had was a note nailed to the door. Now there was a trail to follow. Now there was a clue to chase. Better to take her chances on the ground than let the Snow Merchant escape.

"You're not breaking her promise—just stretching it a bit," said Noah.

That was all the convincing Lettie needed.

"That's right!" she said, pulling off her apron, grabbing her deerskin coat, cramming her fingers into gloves, and tying her boots tight. "Let's go!"

"My hand . . ." murmured the Goggler.

"My head . . ." muttered the Walrus.

As the crones began to stir, Lettie climbed down the ladder and jumped to the ground. She half expected to die right there on the spot, but nothing happened. She felt giddy with shock. Had the danger in Albion all been a lie?

"Come on!" said Noah. "He's got a head start, and longer legs. Follow those frostprints!"

They sprinted down Vinegar Street, following the feet etched in ice upon the cobbles.

The Wind Lends a Hand

Another ninety paces from the White Horse Inn and they were utterly lost. The Snow Merchant's frost-prints led them in circles, crisscrossing and backtracking all over the place.

"He's trying to lose us," said Noah. "He knows we're following him."

"Either that, or he's as lost as we are," said Lettie.

"We haven't caught him up at all. We need a short-cut."

But Lettie didn't know any. Barter looked very different through a telescope. Down here all the street signs were smeared with grime. The cobbles were slippery

with blubber and beer. Gas lamps flickered and died. Underneath them, drunken sailors swore and sang.

"I'm not asking *them* for directions," she said. "They don't know their up from their down."

"What about the Wind?" said Noah.

She rolled her eyes. "You don't expect the *Wind* to show me a shortcut."

"It's *your* friend," said Noah. "It might give you a tug in the right direction."

"Even if I ask, I don't think the Wind will listen."

"It *has* to," he insisted. "That's what joint best friends *do*."

Noah was right, again. If the Wind ignored her now, then it wasn't her friend at all. Closing her eyes and whispering to the air around her, Lettie made a little prayer.

"I don't know if you can hear me, Wind. I don't think you've even got ears. And I know you've not let me go into Barter before, but this is different. I'm lost. I don't know Barter, but you do. You whistle down every street in this town. You can show me a shortcut to the harbor. Please, you've got to."

She took off a glove, held out her hand . . . almost at once, the miracle came. Lettie felt the pull. The pull of the Wind.

It was like an invisible hand had taken hold of hers to lead her someplace. She laughed with the joy of it, she laughed with the wonder. She began to run at such a speed that Noah could barely keep up.

"Where are you going?" he called, and Lettie cried back: "I can feel it! You were right, Noah! Follow me, I know the way!"

The Wind really was talking to her. It had no words; it was speaking in a language of tugs and nudges. Lettie concentrated, feeling the pull, trying to follow where it led. Down side alleys and dark streets, so they could reach the harbor before the Snow Merchant escaped.

The chase was on. And Lettie had discovered a gift, a power: she could hold the hand of the Wind, and it would show the way.

They rushed down backstreets reeking of mold and beer, hopping from one shadow to the next, with Lettie never knowing whether they would go left, right, or straight on. Noah followed Lettie, and Lettie followed the Wind.

They scarpered down Drum Lane; past windows mostly black or curtained, steering clear of the streetlamps. Then Lettie lost the Wind's hand, and they had to crisscross and backtrack before she found

it again. They ran over Riney Bridge, across Swill Street and Pickle Lane. They tiptoed through alleys of nets and rotting rope as the salt smell of the sea grew stronger and stronger. They stopped by a tangled necklace of rigging, strung with bungs of cork.

"Keep running," wheezed Noah. "We've got to catch him."

"Well, I've got to catch my breath first," said Lettie. She leaned against a windowsill gone soft with rot, while her heart raced. Ahead, she heard the tall ship masts rattling in the harbor. She mouthed a *thank you* to the Wind, for saving her life. She still didn't know how the miracle had happened: she was *outside*, having an adventure led by an invisible hand.

"The harbor's just ahead," Lettie said.

"There's not a frostprint in sight!" said Noah. "We've beaten him to it. Let's get to my boat."

The harbor held merchant clippers—big ships with three or four masts and huge rudders—and even some whaling boats with funnels and coal engines. Noah's little wooden ship was squeezed among them. With its single mast and tiny cabin, Lettie wondered how he had managed to sail the world on it. Her mouth must have been hanging open, and Noah must have mistaken her shock for admiration, because he said proudly:

"She's beautiful, isn't she? She's called *Leutha's Wood.* Leutha was my grandmother's name; the ship is made from her stalk."

"She grew all that wood from her shoulder?" Lettie asked.

"Eventually," said Noah. "When my people die, we bury them up to the neck, so the stalk can carry on growing."

"Like a tree!"

"Exactly like a tree," said Noah. "Every one of our forests is the graveyard of a different tribe."

"It sounds like a very different place from Albion." Lettie closed her eyes and tried to imagine. "Strange."

Readying herself to run again, Lettie sprinted for the harbor, and then stopped. The Wind was tugging her *back* to look at a slanted building, leaning heavily against its next-door neighbor, too battered and bruised to stand up on its own. It faced the sea full on, and Lettie could tell that for years it had taken the brunt of the coastal winds, and sailors too drunk or seasick to walk any farther into town. Salt had stripped the paint from the door and the sign that used to hang above it, but Lettie knew the name anyway.

"Why is the Wind bringing me *here?*" she said. "This is the Clam Before the Storm. Da comes here

every night and gambles. He lost nine shillings and sixpence last week. But he didn't have nine shillings and sixpence, so Mr. Sleech, the debt collector, came and took away all the pictures on the walls."

Lettie heard singing coming from inside. She peered through the dirty glass. Inside was a tumbled mess of beer, foam, and giddy sailors. So *this* was where her no-good da spent most of his time. She searched the faces, but couldn't see Da. A group of fishermen fought, a group of whalers drank, and a group of smugglers sang and played a seven-string. It was a famous song that Lettie knew—it told of the love affair between a sailor and an albatross in over a hundred verses. The smugglers were on verse seventy-seven.

"She flew down on the riddled deck.
The moon was full and strange.
She put her wings about his neck,
Her feathers rearranged.
And o! her shape began to change,
Her shape began to change.

"The moon was in her skin and hair,
The stars were in her eyes.
Said she, 'You loved me everywhere

Across the seven seas and skies.
And o! you saw through my disguise,
You saw through my disguise.'"

"I know those whalers," said Noah. "I sell them my roses sometimes, to give to their sweethearts. That's Captain McNulty." He pointed to a red-bearded whaler with bloody gums, picking a fish bone from his teeth with the end of his harpoon.

"Would he help us?" said Lettie. "Is that why the Wind has led us here?"

"He doesn't know how to do much, apart from hunt, kill, and spit."

Lettie pulled a face as Captain McNulty spat the fish bone down the throat of a smuggler holding a high note. He laughed as the poor man choked.

"He's *horrible!*"

"The other whalers aren't much better," said Noah, pointing out each one and naming them. Blubber Johnson was giving one of Noah's polka-dot roses to a girl on his knee and Grot-Nose Charlie was on his seventh pint of ale. The Creechy twins were having a fistfight with the barman. Stoker Pete was arm wrestling three men at once.

"I don't think there's anyone in there who can help,"

said Lettie to Noah, although in truth she wasn't looking at the whalers. She was looking for Da.

Suddenly, the door of the Clam Before the Storm opened, and out flew a man who landed like a sack on the street. Whoever had thrown him stood silhouetted in the doorway.

"We gamble with *shillings* here, Henry, not *pebbles*!" growled the silhouette. "If you don't clear your debts by sunrise, I'll be round to your inn for payment in kind. I've had my eye on your last rug for a while now."

"Yes, Mr. Sleech," said the figure on the street.

The silhouette shut the door.

The man on the street looked at Lettie. It was her da, Henry. He was drunk and red-eyed and his bow tie had been ripped from him. He reeked of ale and tears. It took him a time to recognize her.

"What are you doing here?" he slurred.

The Endless Inflation
of Blüstav the Alchemist

"Promise!" Da said suddenly. He never stammered when he was drunk. "You've broken your promise! You shouldn't be here!"

Lettie faced him, full of anger and dread. "You're not supposed to be here, either! You stay out all night gambling and drinking, and that's not what a da is meant to do!"

Lettie's own words shocked her, because they were true. Once, Da had been there for her. He had taken care of her. But that was years ago.

Did that mean he didn't love her anymore? She thought about whether she loved him back, and she realized that it didn't matter. It didn't matter and she didn't care.

"You're not my da," she said with a lump in her throat. "All you are is trouble."

Lettie stormed off with tears in her eyes—she didn't know where she was going. She was sick of greedy, selfish grown-ups who did nothing but cheat and lie and steal and take her home piece by piece.

"Lettie, come back!" cried Noah.

"Who are these boys?" said Da, rubbing his eyes. "And why are they all speaking at once?"

"Stop talking nonsense," Lettie turned and shouted. "You're drunk!"

She ran to the jetty, Da stumbling after her and Noah following behind, keeping an anxious distance.

"No!" said Da, grabbing her arm. "Well, yes, I *am* drunk. But your ma—"

"If Ma saw you now, she'd box your ears. I'm out here because I met someone who knew her. I'm chasing a clue. What have *you* ever done, all these years? Gamble away our home, bit by bit! You should have been out here, looking for her!"

"Your ma's note says—" he began, his voice trembling.

"You don't believe Ma's note," said Lettie. "You don't believe she's coming back, do you? If you did you'd still tell me stories about her. You'd look after me, and you'd look for her."

Da began to cry; great big drunken tears that spilled over the red rims of his eyes. He sat down—a big sack of beer and debts—with his legs dangling over the edge of the jetty.

"I don't feel well, Lettie."

"Good." She turned her back on him and stared out at the churning sea. "I hope you're sick all over your lucky socks."

"And I'm seeing things too."

"Well, I hope you see Ma and she beats you black and blue."

"No, it's not Ma this time. It's a man. He's walking across the water . . ."

"Well, I hope it's Jesus and he tells you off."

"He's carrying a suitcase."

Lettie whirled round. "Where?"

But she'd already seen him: it was the Snow Merchant, walking over the waves. He had plugged up his mahogany suitcase with newspaper and grease, and he held a pipette of æther. He was using the æther to freeze a path across the sea toward Noah's boat.

"I don't believe it!" said Da. He slapped himself across the face. "I'm hallucinating."

"No, you're not," said Lettie quietly. "I see him too."

She turned and frantically waved at Noah to come over.

Da rubbed his eyes. "No, Lettie, you don't understand. I'm seeing your ma's old master. Master Blüstav. She went off with him one day, and I never saw either of them again. Now here I am, watching him walking across the water. I really have had too much ale. My brain's a muddle . . ."

He shook his head violently.

"That didn't do any good, I'm still seeing him."

"Da, listen . . ." Lettie tried to make sense of him and her own confusion. Blüstav the Snow Merchant, Blüstav the Master Alchemist from the story, Blüstav the con man . . . if Da was talking sense, they were all the same person.

And he was getting away!

"Da, listen!" she yelled, taking him by the shoulder and shaking him. *"Blüstav's really there!"*

"Impossible!" said Da.

"He is. I see him!"

"Me too!" said Noah, arriving beside her.

Da's eyes widened. In them was something that Lettie had not seen for years and years.

Hope.

"Blüstav!" he called. "Blüstav! Where's Teresa?"

Blüstav didn't hear. He pushed his suitcase up onto the jetty and crept toward *Leutha's Wood.*

"He's not stopping!" said Da. "He's running off, the scoundrel! Come back, you crook! What have you done with Teresa?"

Lettie wanted answers too. With the Wind tugging her along, her feet clunking on wooden planks, she raced down the jetty toward *Leutha's Wood.*

"Blüstav!" Da shouted. "Where's Teresa?"

"Where's Ma?" Lettie found herself yelling.

Now that Blüstav had heard the shouts, he began running as fast as he could. But his mahogany suitcase weighed him down and they caught up with him quickly. He slowed to a stop, gasping for breath.

"We've got you trapped," said Da.

Blüstav smiled. He coolly picked a frozen bead of sweat from his forehead and flicked it into the sea. A hand came out from his coat holding something. Lettie saw it too late. The bottle of gastromajus!

She yelped and jumped away, pulling at Da and Noah.

But Blüstav was too quick. He tipped the pink alchemical right down Da's throat. Da fell back on the jetty, spluttering and gasping.

"That'll teach you to trap an alchemist," said Blüstav.

"What did you just do?" Lettie gasped, heart thumping. "He's my da!"

"Not for long," said Blüstav.

She gave him her most furious glare.

Blüstav's hand twitched.

Perhaps he was thinking about tipping some gastro-majus over Lettie, too.

"I wouldn't if I were you," said Noah, snapping a huge thorn from his stalk and holding it like a dagger.

Blüstav shrugged, turned, and fled toward *Leutha's Wood*.

"Come back!" Lettie roared. "You come back!"

She turned to where Da lay on the planks, gasping and pulling at his red hair. "What's happening to you?" she said.

As if in answer, Da began to change.

It was the most frightening thing she'd ever seen. The alchemy was turning her da into a . . . what? His neck was stretching up and up and his skin was turning see-through green. And all the while he was shrinking, shrinking down. The air popped and crackled, and smoke began streaming from his ears and mouth. For a moment, Lettie was blinded. She waved her hands, coughing. Noah pulled her away from the green smoke and sparks.

Together, they looked down at Da. Lettie could scarcely believe what he'd become. She reached out to touch him and felt glass. It was smooth and cool. It was real. It had really happened.

Da had just turned into a corked bottle of beer.

Scooping up Da in her hand, Lettie chased after Blüstav.

Reaching *Leutha's Wood*, Blüstav heaved his suitcase aboard and began unwinding the rope mooring the ship to the jetty, trying to set sail.

Lettie and Noah weren't going to let that happen.

They jumped on deck as Blüstav wrestled with the rigging. Noah had his thorn, and Lettie had a plan.

Blüstav turned around, glaring. He rummaged in his deep pockets for his bottle of gastromajus.

But he had to find it first.

Lettie knew she had a few seconds before they were both turned into the contents of their last meal, and she made them count. As he whipped out the alchemical, she jumped for the suitcase.

"Stop that!" Blüstav shrieked.

But Lettie's fingers were already wrapped around the rags jamming the holes, and with a sucking sound she tugged them out.

Blüstav pushed her away with his one free hand and

she fell on the deck, hard. But the cloud was already spilling into the night. It was too late for Blüstav to plug the hole with his thumbs.

"You stupid girl!" he shrieked, dropping his bottle of gastromajus to the floor.

"Let that be a lesson to you," said Noah, scooping it up. "*No one* tries to steal my grandmother."

Blüstav ignored him. He was trying desperately to waft the two wisps of cloud back into his suitcase, but it was useless. More and more of the nimbostratus leaked out.

"Give up," said Lettie. "You've lost!"

"I never lose!" Blüstav snarled. "Snow is mine, and I'll never let it go!"

Frantically, Blüstav buttoned up his long coat to the neck and tucked the hem into his socks. Bewildered, she watched as he pulled the sleeves until they extended far past his bony fingers. Then he heaved the mahogany chest close and covered each hole with a sleeve. The snow cloud was still drifting out of the holes, but now it was funneling into his coat, which began to swell up like an inflating balloon.

"I see what you're up to!" Noah said. He jumped forward, but the alchemist pushed him away easily and laughed.

"Snow belongs to me, and it always will!" he cried, his coat bulging around him. "Try taking it from me *now*!"

Blüstav gave a smile that said *I've won.*

Lettie saw why: now he hovered a finger's breadth above the deck, and he was rising.

And *rising*!

"That'll teach you to trap an alchemist!" he cried, feet kicking the air, the nimbostratus lifting him higher. "I *always* escape!"

Up he went, Blüstav the balloon . . .

Lettie looked on, dumbstruck and defeated, while Noah jumped and caught hold of Blüstav's boot. But still the nimbostratus surged upward, taking Noah along too.

"What are you *doing*?" spat Blüstav.

"What *are* you doing?" Lettie echoed.

"Rope, Lettie!" he cried. "Rope!"

Lettie grabbed a length of rigging coiled in a pile and threw it to Noah. Lashing her end to the mahogany and lead suitcase, Noah tied his to Blüstav. With a jerk, the rope went taut and the alchemist hung in the air, suspended and swaying, with Noah holding on to his boots.

Blüstav was a strange sight, coat puffed up, arms

and legs wriggling. He swore and cursed, but Lettie could only smile as the cloud in his coat rumbled, and he flashed blue.

"Not that good at escaping, are you, Blüstav?" she giggled.

Blüstav yelped as the angry cloud thundered inside his coat.

"You—*AH!*—stupid—*AH!*—girl!"

"Blüstav the balloon," Noah said, dropping back to the deck.

"Now we've caught him *and* the nimbostratus. That was quick thinking, Noah."

They both stood, gasping with adrenaline and exhaustion. After a while they began to laugh. It was half-past midnight. The new day was minutes old, and already they had stopped a robbery, run with the Wind, trapped an alchemist, and rescued a grandmother. And now, finally, Lettie was going to get some answers.

"You've got a lot of explaining to do, Blüstav."

"I think," he said, bobbing nervously, "that before I do that—*AH!*—you should cast off."

And he looked down the jetty.

To where the Goggler and the Walrus were coming *clomp clomp clomp* over the boards, toward *Leutha's Wood*.

"Oh, no," said Noah.

The Goggler had stuffed one hand into her pocket. It jangled faintly with loose change. In the other, she held the last silver pistol. The Walrus's head was steaming with anger and tea. It was hatred that had a hold on them now, Lettie realized, as much as greed.

"They don't just want the snow cloud," she said. "They're out to get revenge."

"So am I, when this nimbostratus stops—*AH!*—electrocuting me," replied Blüstav through gritted teeth. "But for now, I suggest we escape, *together*."

"Why don't we just leave you behind?" said Noah, jabbing at Blüstav with his thorn.

Blüstav, though his hair stood on end and his teeth buzzed with electricity, tried his best to smile.

"If you throw me overboard, Lettie will never know what I know about her mother."

Noah scowled. "That's why you revealed you knew her, so if you were caught, you'd have something to bargain with."

"Ma, me, and snow," said Lettie. "I want to know everything. *Everything*, Blüstav. Do you swear?"

He nodded frantically. "Yes, yes, I—*AH!*—I swear!"

The crones were close enough to shout now. The

Goggler cursed Blüstav in Bohemian and the Walrus cursed in Laplöndi.

"Do we have—*AH!*—a deal?!" he shrieked.

Lettie looked at her da; a green bottle in her hands. She looked at the Walrus and the Goggler running toward them, greedy and vengeful. She looked at Noah. He looked back and nodded.

Lettie gulped. "It's a deal, Blüstav. Now let's get out of here."

And all at once—the Wind began to blow.

PART TWO
Upon the Sea

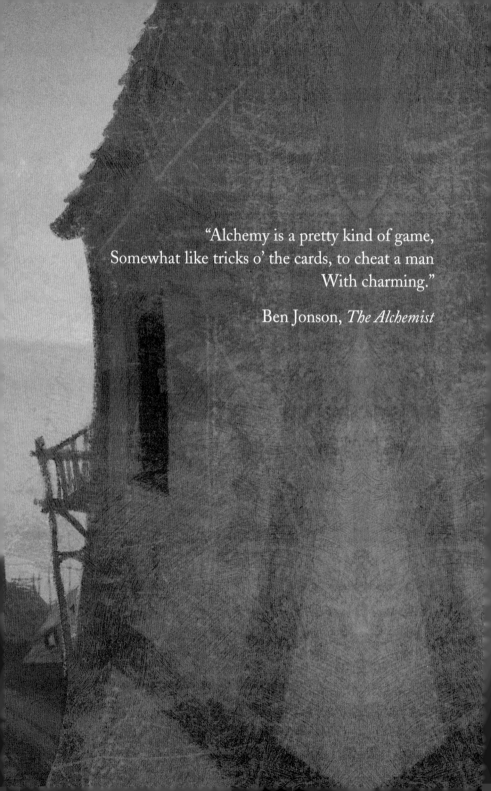

"Alchemy is a pretty kind of game,
Somewhat like tricks o' the cards, to cheat a man
With charming."

Ben Jonson, *The Alchemist*

❦ CONTENTS ❧

Shaking Out the Truth

It was one o'clock on a blustery Albion morning. The moon was the color of rust, and the sea was the color of coal as *Leutha's Wood* drifted from the harbor into the world beyond. It was Lettie's first time at sea. Standing on deck, watching the lights of Pickle Lane and Vinegar Street fade and disappear, she wondered where they were heading.

They were picking up speed.

"Noah? Why are you unfurling the sail?"

"The Wind has helped us so far," he shouted, pulling on the rigging and tying complicated knots. "And something tells me those old crones aren't going to give up that easily."

Lettie shivered in her deerskin coat. He was right. The Walrus and the Goggler hungered for snow and they would never stop until it was theirs.

"The Wind will steer the ship," said Noah. "I'll take care of the sails, and you can deal with Blüstav!"

Lettie grimaced. That was the one good thing: at least they had the alchemist trapped.

"Do you want to give me your da?" said Noah. "I think I've got a shelf I can stick him on. He'll be safer there."

Lettie handed Da over and Noah took him inside. Then she looked up at Blüstav. The cloud wasn't so stormy now and he bobbed on his string, glaring at her.

"Those crones will come after us, you know," she said. "They want the snow cloud all to themselves."

"They can't have it!" he snapped. "Neither can you! It's mine! *Argh!*"

The cloud rumbled. A spark crawled across his coat like a blue spider.

"We've got a deal, Blüstav. Tell me the truth. Why come here to give me snow? What has this got to do with Ma?"

"Everything," he answered miserably. "Everything. This is all her fault."

Lettie trembled. She looked at him fiercely. *"Tell me."*

"Where to begin?" said Blüstav. "What do you know about your mother?"

Lettie hardly dared breathe; afraid she might miss a word. "I know her name was Teresa, and she lost a game of chess to my da, and she was learning the pianola, and she built our inn with alchemy. I've got her eyes."

"And her coat," said Blüstav. "She was wearing that the day we met. Listen, girl, I came to sell you snow for one simple reason: you are Teresa Peppercorn's daughter. She was stubborn, smart, and questioning, just like you. And, when I first met her, she was in a lot of trouble."

Blüstav paused, and Lettie could see a *quickness* in his eyes. A craftiness.

"I rescued her," he continued. "We were in Petrossia, you see, prisoners of the czar. An hour away from execution, we were. But, of course, the czar couldn't keep a master alchemist like me in a cell for long—"

At once the Wind interrupted him with an angry gust.

He tried to carry on: "When we escaped from Petrossia I made her my apprentice and taught her everything I knew"—the Wind blew hard again, and Blüstav began to pirouette on his rope—"but then she betrayed *meeeeeeeeeeeeeeeeeEEE*!!"

Blüstav couldn't continue his story: the Wind wouldn't let him. It gusted around him; it twirled him in the air like a weather vane.

"Stop it!" he begged, spinning round and round, his face a queasy blur. "Help me! Let me down!"

"Leave him alone!" Lettie scolded the Wind. "Let him speak!"

She started to pull Blüstav down out of the Wind, but Noah stopped her.

"It's angry because he's *lying*," Noah said. "Not because he's *speaking*."

At once Lettie understood. Of *course* Blüstav was lying—to him it was as natural as breathing! Somehow, the Wind knew, and it was trying to shake the truth out of him. She should have known herself: his eyes were easier to read now that the æther was wearing off.

Lettie Peppercorn, you gullible fool!

"Right!" she shouted. "That's *enough*!"

The Wind stopped. A whimpering Blüstav bobbed on his rope.

"I'm *sick* of lies," said Lettie. "Sick! And if you lie

again, I'll let the Wind blow until *you're* sick too!"

Blüstav's mouth opened and closed, but he had nothing to say.

"Every time you bend the truth, every time you twist it, or spin away from it, the Wind will twist and spin *you*." Lettie sat down on the deck and made herself comfortable. "And that's how it's going to be. For as long as it takes the truth to come. Understand?"

Blüstav nodded.

And he began slowly—for the first time in his life—to tell the truth.

The Making of Snow

Blüstav and Teresa met in an underground prison, somewhere in Petrossia. The prison belonged to the czar, ruler of that dark land of forests. They had both been sentenced to die in a horribly gruesome way, involving nothing but a teaspoon and two barrels of beetroot soup.

The czar had Blüstav in chains for "borrowing" alchemy books from one of his rivals, and "forgetting" to give them back.

Teresa had also committed a crime involving alchemy. She had changed the czar's son, the Prince of Petrossia, into a cat.

"I saw him kick a dog on the street," Teresa explained.

"I thought the dog might like to get its own back."

Blüstav was naturally suspicious of this brown-haired girl with fierce eyes. None of the alchemical books he'd ever "borrowed" had told him how to change a person into a cat. They were all about making gold. He decided that Teresa must be a liar, which made him uneasy. Being a liar himself, he knew how troublesome they could be. It was not until they were an hour away from their terrible execution that he realized Teresa was, in fact, telling the truth (which meant too that she was a genius).

They were chained by shackles of lead to a cold stone floor, listening to the dank walls drip, when Teresa turned to him and said, "You're an alchemist, aren't you?"

"The greatest now living," lied Blüstav.

"I want to be an alchemist," said Teresa. "I want to turn pebbles into pigeons and walnuts into whales."

Blüstav naturally assumed that, as well as lying, Teresa liked to tell jokes. He laughed.

"Girl, an alchemist dedicates himself to one thing: turning lead into gold. Understand? An alchemist wants to become rich. Alchemy is the science of greed."

"Well, most alchemists have no imagination at all. I want to make things far more wonderful than gold."

Blüstav clicked his tongue in irritation. What was more

wonderful than wealth? "Have you read Dorn's Philosophia Speculativa?" he asked. "Or Ovid's Metamorphoses? Have you read Zetzner's Theatrum Chemicum?"

"No."

"Then you will never be an alchemist," said Blüstav. "It takes a lifetime of study, and you're going to die in an hour."

"Well," said Teresa. "Why don't you save our lives, then?"

"Impossible!" Blüstav declared, and Teresa shook her head in irritation, as if she disliked the word.

"Why is it impossible?" she asked. "Your alchemy could save us."

"My alchemy? True, I could change these lead chains into gold ones," Blüstav lied, "but what help would that be? We still couldn't escape!"

"What if I saved us?" asked Teresa. "Then could I be your apprentice? You could teach me what Mr. Dorn and Mr. Ovid and Mr. Zetzner have to say."

Blüstav sighed: this girl was a liar, a comedian, and a fool. He closed his eyes. "Some things you just can't change. A death sentence is one of them."

"Everything changes," said Teresa. "I'll show you."

Then she began to experiment, mashing up moss and limestone with other ingredients lying around the cell;

things Blüstav could no longer remember. In a few minutes Teresa had made a discovery.

"This should do it," she muttered, smearing the paste over their shackles, which began to hiss and change.

As Blüstav watched in amazement, they turned green and sprouted yellow and white flowers. Binding his hands were no longer lead chains, but daisy chains.

"See?" said Teresa, ripping them off. "Easy. Now let's do the same to the bars on that window!"

Half an hour later they were running down a muddy track, the shouting of the guards far behind. A breathless Blüstav knew two things: he was no longer going to die, and his new apprentice was already the greatest alchemist ever to have lived.

And he realized something else: she could make him a fortune.

When they got back to his laboratory, Blüstav showed Teresa around.

"There are three things all alchemists must have in their laboratory. Number one: shelves!"

"Why, Master Blüstav?" said Teresa.

"They are where you will neatly stack your alchemicals. Number two: a cauldron!"

"Why, Master Blüstav?"

"The cauldron is where you will mix your alchemicals. Finally, number three: a library of rare and mysterious books!"

"What do I do with those?"

"You sit there and look at them and think how clever they have made you."

Then he gestured to the laboratory around him: to the stove and bellows, the water pump, the armchairs and the window. "Everything else," he said, clapping his hands together, "is a luxury. Now! I am going to test you, Teresa. It is the same test my master gave me when I first became his apprentice. I want you to change that cauldron into . . ." Blüstav settled on the first thing that came into his mind. "Gold. A great, big pile of gold."

"Why, Master Blüstav?"

What irritated Blüstav most about Teresa was that she asked so many questions. Particularly that short little one. It was such an easy question to ask, but it required him to make up the most complicated answers.

Because it will make me rich, *he thought excitedly.*

"Because it will teach you alchemy," he said solemnly.

"But I already know how to make gold," said Teresa. "It's boring yellow stuff. Teach me something else."

Blüstav gritted his teeth. He would have to find some other way to make his fortune from Teresa.

"Very well," he said. "Turn the cauldron into a . . ."

His mind skipped through various possibilities: Chicken? Egg? Clock? Dressing gown? Lampshade?

"A boat," he settled on eventually.

Teresa went over to the library of books, and studied the titles on the spines. "They're all about making gold."

Blüstav chuckled. Did she expect one to be called How to Change Cauldrons into Boats?

After a while Teresa walked away from the shelves.

Blüstav was disappointed. "At least have a go," he said.

"I am," said Teresa.

She turned on the water pump, flooded the laboratory, and got in the cauldron.

"Finished," she said. "The cauldron is now a boat."

"That's cheating!" said Blüstav, furious that Teresa had both outwitted him and got his feet wet.

"That's using your imagination," she corrected.

"Imagination has no place in the mind of an alchemist," Blüstav declared.

Teresa sighed. "But, Master, alchemy happens in your head before it happens anywhere else."

From that day, Blüstav began planning how to exploit Teresa. He wanted to trick her into making him rich, but she was too gifted, stubborn, and questioning just to turn lead into gold for him. Blüstav needed a lie more devious than any he had ever told before.

This was it: "Teresa! I am going to give you more tests: each one will be difficult in its own way. Trust in your master. Once you have completed all the tests, you will become the world's greatest alchemist."

However, beneath Blüstav's lie was a plan: every alchemical potion Teresa made, he would sell to the rich and famous. It was the greatest lie of his life, and Teresa believed it totally.

So Blüstav traveled the world, talking to the rich and the powerful, and they told him their desires:

"I want a seven-fingered hand," said a concert violinist in Edenborg. "I'll pay you in gold."

"I want diamonds on the soles of these shoes," said the Duke of Madri. "I'll pay you in silver."

"I want flea lotion for my son," said the Czar of Petrossia. "I'll pay you in platinum."

Teresa's alchemy fulfilled their every wish, and in return, Blüstav took their gold and silver and platinum. His customers all agreed that truly, he was the Greatest Alchemist of his Age, and not one of them suspected that all the while it was his apprentice who worked his incredible alchemy.

The lie couldn't last. Blüstav, obsessed by his fortune of gold and silver and platinum, didn't notice Teresa changing. But she was. Every Tuesday, Thursday, and Saturday, she would glance out the window to a patch of well-trodden grass below. She smiled for no reason at all. It was only when she started making mistakes, and Blüstav's reputation as the Greatest Alchemist of his Age began to suffer, that he finally noticed what was happening.

"TERESA!"

"What, Master?"

"You gave the Prince of Baveria the legs of a scorpion and the tail of a horse!"

"Oh," said Teresa. "Isn't that what he wanted?"

"It was the other way around!" shouted Blüstav. "He's got a very important war to fight and now even his own soldiers are laughing at him! You've just lost me a very important and incredibly wealthy customer!"

"Oh," said Teresa. "Oh, well."

Then she gave a long sigh and looked out the window.

"My goodness," said Blüstav. "You're in love!" It was so obvious now that he wondered how he hadn't seen it before.

"That's right," said Teresa, showing him the ring. "And married too."

"Married?" Blüstav yelled. "When? To whom?"

"At two o'clock this morning, to my husband," said Teresa. "I can't be your apprentice anymore, Master, I'm Mrs. Peppercorn now. I quit!"

Those two words terrified Blüstav. He froze, as if a lion had prowled into the room. If Teresa left, he'd lose everything! Fortune! Reputation! He pleaded and threatened; he called her names until he lost his voice.

"You haven't completed all your tests!" he cried. "You'll never be the Greatest Alchemist now! Stay, Teresa, your master commands it!"

But Teresa wouldn't listen. Lies had no effect on her anymore: she was in love, and that was the truth.

Blüstav stared out of the window as she left, feeling numb.

And then a single thought formed in his mind: one day, he would have his revenge.

Time passed, and Blüstav sank into misery, poverty, and obscurity. His customers forgot him. He forgot the few bits of alchemy he had once known. He couldn't create anything. He couldn't even invent a decent plan of revenge.

Blüstav was sitting around in his laboratory, staring up at his shelves of alchemicals and books, waiting for *inspiration, when it happened. There was a knock at the door.*

"Is that you, Teresa?"

"It's me!" she called through the letterbox. "I have lots of alchemy to do. Will you help?"

"Of course I will," Blüstav lied. "What is it for?"

"It's for my daughter, Lettie. It's going to save her life."

Blüstav felt himself filling up with jealousy. This was the first time Teresa had made something that wasn't his.

"What is it?" he asked, and he knew before she told him that he wanted it.

"A new invention," said Teresa. "Snow."

Teresa needed a new laboratory—a cold place, away from dry land. So she and Blüstav sailed across the Channel, found an iceberg, and hollowed out a laboratory in the top, complete with cauldron. They painted all the walls with æther to keep in the cold.

"That's the easy part," Teresa told Blüstav. "Now the real work begins."

Blüstav realized Teresa was in the middle of alchemy so complicated he didn't even understand what it was she was changing, let alone why she was doing it. He slunk around the iceberg, little more than a servant, fetching whatever she asked. And all the while he waited for his chance.

A year passed as if it were a day. Teresa made a great silver wheel, and on it she spun a cloud. In great glass tubes the shape of bells she grew shining white ice.

One night as Teresa worked on her invention, Blüstav crept up to the laboratory and found her asleep from exhaustion. She had cut a length of silence one hundred years long into tiny moments, charged them with static and coated them with dust. She had sewn them inside a cloud, and thrown in six dice six times over. She had stirred in salt and æther. Above her head floated the nimbostratus, so nearly finished. Only one final ingredient remained.

Blüstav went to the recipe she held in her hand and gently took it from her grasp. He read the last instruction, for it was the only one he understood.

"'Finally, add water,'" he murmured.

Teresa slept on, as he filled up a bucket and threw it into the cloud. He stepped back as the first snowflakes fell.

"Diamonds," breathed Blüstav. "She's found a way to turn water into diamonds."

To him, this was more incredible than turning lead into gold. The greed inside him stirred again, like a *hibernating beast after a long winter. He wanted the snow more than anything. And it was then that, lacking any imagination, Blüstav thought about stealing it. What else could he do? All his life he had been a thief. His palms itched, and suddenly he was holding a handful of the diamonds in his hand.*

They melted away to water.

"It's just water," he said, crestfallen. He almost laughed: for the first time, Teresa had tricked him, and she had done it in her sleep.

Then Blüstav realized: if snow had fooled him, it could trick other people too. If he took the cloud, he could sell the snow as "diamonds," then escape before they melted. It would be a lie that would give Blüstav both the fortune and the revenge he craved.

He didn't stop to think about Teresa's daughter, and why she needed snow to live.

With Teresa slumped over her desk, asleep, Blüstav packed the cloud inside a suitcase. He stuffed as many alchemicals as he could carry in his coat pockets, and crept out of the laboratory. Softly, he shut the doors, took several steps backward, and searched his pockets for one of the æther vials he had stolen.

He threw it, hard. A hundred drops of liquid frost burst upon the doors. They scattered over the hinges, the handles, the lock; the æther froze them shut in seconds. It would be a long, long time before they thawed.

Blüstav smiled at the thought of Teresa trapped in her laboratory. It was fitting revenge for what she had done to him. He went down the stairs to the jetty and set off in the only rowboat for the shore.

He didn't look back, not once.

The Distant Rising Smoke

"That was ten years ago," said Blüstav. "Ever since then, I've traveled all over the world from city to city. I arrive, fill my customers up with æther, pretend to sell them diamonds . . . and vanish with their money before the snow melts."

All through his story, Lettie's hatred for Blüstav had been building up inside her like steam. He had stolen, tricked, and marooned Ma on an iceberg laboratory. He was the most deceitful and selfish person she had ever known.

And he didn't even care!

"What made you come to me?" she growled.

Blüstav gave a greedy smile, but his eyes were troubled. This time Lettie read his gaze easily, seeing that same *quickness* in them as before. They were searching his head for a reply.

No, not a reply, thought Lettie. *A lie. He's looking for a lie to tell me.*

And for a moment, that struck her as strange. But just then Blüstav found his lie:

"It was an experiment, I suppose."

It wasn't a very good lie, but he spoke it with such sincerity it made Lettie forget, at least for a while, the truth: Blüstav didn't really know *why* he had brought snow to Lettie.

"Yes, an experiment. I thought you might unlock the secret of snow. After ten years I still don't know what it really *does*, except melt. I thought perhaps the truth might make me even richer."

"I see," said Lettie, not really seeing.

"The mystery of snow was yours to solve. It was made for you, Lettie Peppercorn. Now it's mine, but in the beginning, it was yours."

"Well, now you can give it *back*!" Lettie shouted.

"Snow melts for you, the same as it melts for everyone else," Blüstav said scornfully. "Why should I?"

Lettie didn't have an answer. Why was she so special? How exactly could snow save her life? Only Ma knew. If only she was there! Lettie clenched her fists and jammed them in her coat. It was so frustrating. What were they supposed to do now?

She stood there wondering until Noah came up to her. "The Wind's still blowing us away from Albion. Shall I draw in the sails? Or do you want to ask it where we're going?"

Lettie looked at him sideways. "Do you really believe the Wind is leading me places? I don't even know if I believe that myself."

"It's not the strangest thing about you," said Noah. "You live in a house on stilts, where spoons change to twigs. You've had an invention made for you called snow, and your joint best friend is a pigeon."

"I suppose so."

"Of course!" He looked up at the sail, taut and white against the dark sky. "I'm a sailor, Lettie, I go where the Wind takes me. And it led me to you, didn't it? I was born ten thousand miles away, but the Wind brought me to Barter, and now we're friends. We're on this boat for a *reason*."

"You're right, Noah. It helped us catch Blüstav, rescued us from the Walrus and the Goggler, and now it's leading us somewhere else."

"But where? Can you ask?"

Lettie frowned and shook her head. "It doesn't really work like that. I can talk, I can ask questions, but the only answer is a tug in the right direction."

"Oh," Noah said. "But what question have you asked, Lettie?"

Lettie turned to watch the waves rush past, sending up spray. "Where's Ma?" she whispered. "That's the question, Noah. Da doesn't know. Neither does Blüstav."

Noah nodded. "But the Wind does."

"How can it know?"

Noah shrugged. "It just does. And soon, we will too."

Lettie had a strange feeling in her chest. Since before she could remember, there had been an emptiness inside her, like a hunger. Now, for the first time in her life, she felt it shrinking. She hugged herself and shut her eyes.

"Are you all right, Lettie?" said Noah.

She nodded. "I just really hope we're going to find Ma, because now that I've started thinking about her, I can't stop."

"We are," said Noah. "I know we are."

"What is that, over there?" said Blüstav up above.

"What is what? Over where?" said Lettie.

Blüstav pointed back in the direction of Albion.

Rising from the sea was a black line. Lettie watched in fascination as it drew up and up. Then another line started the same way: scribbling on the blank slate of sky, like God was writing a message.

"Two," she counted. "No, three. What are they?"

The lines began to smudge at the end, and she realized what they were.

"Smoke plumes," said Noah.

Heart hammering, Lettie fumbled in her pocket for her telescope. "Smoke means funnels and funnels mean a ship and a ship means . . ."

She put an eye to the telescope.

"It's a whaling boat from Barter," she said to Noah.

Four Drops of Æther

"What's the ship's name?" Noah asked grimly. "Is it the *Bloodbucket*?"

Lettie looked for the name, splashed in white paint across the rusty hull. "Yes."

"That's Captain McNulty's boat; he's the whaler we saw in the Clam Before the Storm."

"I know." Lettie could see the red-bearded captain on his deck, standing next to . . . the Walrus and the Goggler.

"The crones are there too, aren't they?" said Noah.

Lettie nodded. "We knew they wouldn't give up. They're chasing us."

"I'm done for!" wailed Blüstav, his face white with fright, as well as frost.

"We *all* are," said Lettie. "Noah, can we get away?"

Noah bit his lip. "I thought we'd get more time."

"I know!" she cried. "I'll ask the Wind to blow them back to the jetty!"

Noah shook his head. "The Wind can't stop them, Lettie. They have propellers, and engines, and big piles of coal to stoke in a furnace."

Lettie knew what he was saying: there was no escape. She needed a plan, and she needed it now.

"What do I do?" she whispered.

Lettie tried to feel the pull of the Wind, but she could only feel it tickling her nose. Maybe she had a cold coming on. She shook herself and tried to concentrate, but it was impossible. There had to be a thousand sneezes stuffed up there! And as the tickling grew, so did an idea in Lettie's head.

Lettie Peppercorn, that's mad!

But the idea stayed with her all the same, niggling away.

Maybe. Just maybe . . .

She dug around in the corners of her pockets for anything she could find: dried spice, old coriander, chili. Her fingers rolled over something coarse and round: a single peppercorn.

Lettie smiled. That would do. It might be an impossible plan, but it was worth a try.

She had the peppercorn, now she needed one more thing.

"Blüstav!" she called up to him. She paused. "I'd ask you politely, but I don't have time. Give me your æther!"

"An alchemist *never* surrenders his potions," Blüstav sneered.

"I thought that's what you'd say," she smiled, motioning to Noah. Together they took hold of the rope tethering him and began to reel him in. Blüstav wriggled and whined, but he was helpless to stop her from plucking the æther bottle from his pocket. Noah let go of Blüstav and he soared back into the air, bobbing on the end of his rope like a cork in water.

"Thank you," said Lettie, shaking the vial. There didn't seem to be much left. She unscrewed the lid, hoping it would be enough.

"Are you sure you know what you're doing, Lettie?" asked Noah.

"No," she said. "But here goes, anyway."

She stuck out her tongue and squeezed a drop of

æther from the pipette. It was like swallowing all of winter. The numbness tumbled down her throat, and the warmth around her heart vanished.

"Stop it, Lettie!"

"What's going on?" wailed Blüstav from above. "If you use up the last of my æther, I'll start defrosting! My snow cloud will be *ruined*. The slightest change in temperature can be *disastrous*. Once, in the tropics, it heated up ever so slightly and made nothing but thunderstorms for a week."

Lettie ignored him and drank another drop. Her heart beat and beat like it wanted to leave her chest. Her knees shook, her teeth chattered, and ice began to form between her toes.

"Halfway there," she muttered.

A third drop. Little icicles were forming, starting from her eyebrows and down over her eyes.

"Just one more . . ."

"Don't!" said Noah. "One more drop, and you'll never be warm again."

"Don't be stupid, girl," called Blüstav. "No one's ever taken that much æther."

Noah grabbed her shoulder, trying to take the bottle from her. He yelped as if he'd been stung: Lettie was already freezing.

But it wasn't enough. She had to be *more* than freezing, colder than even Blüstav.

"Just g-g-get the hot-water b-b-bottle ready when I get b-back," she managed.

And her fingers squeezed the pipette, and the fourth drop fell.

It was the worst feeling she'd ever felt. Her bones were brittle as glass, her blood barely moved in her veins. There was not a shiver of warmth in her whole body. All the heat had been squeezed out and now she felt nothing but the grip of the cold, the cold, the cold . . .

She dropped the almost-empty bottle into her pocket and stepped toward the side of the boat. She jumped the rail and tumbled overboard.

"Save her!" she heard Noah shout. "She'll drown, she'll freeze, she'll die."

Lettie realized he was pleading not with Blüstav but with the Wind. She tried to speak, to tell him it was all right that this was part of her plan, but there was not enough time. She hit the waves with a slap.

Lettie hit the waves but didn't sink. She skipped across them like a stone, until she tumbled, bounced, and skidded to a rest, her eyes frozen shut.

Lettie Peppercorn, don't you die, she told herself.

It took her a while to pick away the ice gluing her eyelids shut. When she finally opened them, she saw the sky. She lay on her back. Struggling up onto her elbows, Lettie looked around her and managed a smile. Her plan had worked!

She hadn't sunk into the sea: she had *frozen* it.

At her touch, the waves directly below her had turned to ice. Shakily, she got to her feet and stood on her little island of frozen sea, looking up at *Leutha's Wood*. Noah leaned over the rail, staring openmouthed, holding an inflatable life ring. She still couldn't speak, so, as fast as her frozen body would allow, she lifted her hand and waved.

"Lettie Peppercorn, get back up here!" said Noah. He was trying to be angry, but he just sounded relieved.

Lettie shook her head, turning toward the *Bloodbucket*. She wondered if walking was a sensible idea, but it didn't really matter either way. She had to try. She put one foot lightly on a wave. It froze before she even stepped on to it. She exuded the cold, like an aura. The ice was slippery but firm.

She took another step, then another. It was hard walking with the ground constantly shifting beneath her feet, but she was doing it. She was walking across the water.

"Wait there!" called Noah. "You're walking the wrong way!"

Of course I am, she thought. *Someone's got to get rid of those old ladies.*

She began to head across the sea, toward the *Bloodbucket.*

An Itchy Nose Saves the Day

With the Wind roaring in her ears, Lettie bounded over the waves and skittered across the swells. Skipping was the fastest way to move, she quickly found. Up ahead, the *Bloodbucket* drew closer. It bristled with funnels, trailing smoke. Its iron hull had a harpoon gun bolted to the front and a great crane—for lifting dead whales into the cargo hold—saddled on the side. From every plank and rivet came the stink of rot and blood.

The crones stood on deck. The Goggler looked through her scopical glasses, while the Walrus held on to an oversized wig that covered her spout and the hole in her teapot head.

Lettie drew up to the side of the ship. The stench was so strong she could taste it. Her stomach clenched like a fist and she gagged. She wished she was back on *Leutha's Wood*, with Noah taking care of her. Cups of khave, thick blankets, and hot-water bottles . . . The yearning for warmth inside her was so strong that she had to choke back a sob. She held the peppercorn in her hand. She couldn't afford to cry, not if this was going to work.

The engines whirred and sputtered and died as the ship slid to a stop. The *Bloodbucket* was eerily silent. Lettie peered into a porthole studding the side. She jumped: a sudden face appeared on the other side of the glass. It was coal-blackened Stoker Pete, scowling at her.

Lettie stepped away and looked up at the deck, trying to speak, but her jaw was still frozen shut. Eventually, though, her chattering teeth worked her mouth open, and she managed a: "H-H-Helloooooo!"

A man with bloody gums and a wiry red beard leaned over the side, scrutinizing her through a huge telescope.

"Whatever it is," said Captain McNulty, "'tis *alive!*"

"I'm n-not an 'it'—" began Lettie.

Captain McNulty grinned and spat something green into the sea. "And it *talks.*"

A voice said: "It's a mermaid, then."

"Blubber Johnson, stop your postulatin'," said Captain McNulty. "It ain't no mermaid, it ain't got a tail. Looks like a young girl."

Another voice said hopefully: "Aye? A beautiful young girl?"

"Nay, rather plain," Captain McNulty answered. "Come see for yerself."

There were several clanging steps, and a sailor whose nose was swollen with carbuncles and pustules leaned over the rail to squint at Lettie. He said: "Then it ain't no sea siren. Sea sirens be very beautiful."

"Get back to yer post, Grot-Nose Charlie," Captain McNulty muttered, and the other sailor vanished.

Lettie glared at the captain. "I'm not a mermaid, I'm not a sea siren, and I'm not plain: I'm Lettie Peppercorn, and I want to speak to your passengers."

Captain McNulty polished the end of his telescope vigorously, and studied Lettie further. "Lettie Peppercorn? So you are," he said. He turned and called: "We found yer landlady! She's bright blue!"

Lettie gulped as the Goggler and the Walrus appeared over the side. Their eyes were truly terrible now: red with rage and no sleep, green with greed and seasickness. Lettie stared back as bravely as she could.

"Grab her with the crane!" cried the Goggler with glee. "Grab her!" With her remaining hand, she made pincer movements.

Lettie saw that almost all the gold rings had vanished from the old crones' fingers. So that was what the Whalers were being paid with: gold. Lettie wondered if there was a grown-up alive who didn't care about getting rich.

"Grot-Nose Charlie!" screamed Captain McNulty. "Bring her up!"

Grot-Nose Charlie worked the levers, and the crane creaked and swung toward Lettie. The rusted claw lowered down toward her and tried to pluck her from the waves. But Grot-Nose Charlie was used to fishing dead things from the sea, and he couldn't catch Lettie as she skipped backward and out of reach.

"I'd rather stay where I am, thank you."

The Goggler narrowed her eyes and whipped out her silver pistol. She flicked down a lens on her scopical glasses with black crosshairs painted upon it. "*We* are in charge here! *You* are our prisoner!"

"Careful!" warned the Walrus. "She's taken æther. She's up to something."

Yes I am, thought Lettie. In her hand she crushed the dried peppercorn between the pestle and mortar of her frozen thumb and palm, grinding it into a fine dust.

Keep them talking, she thought. *Just a little longer.*

"I know you want the snow cloud . . ." she began.

"Of course we do!" cried the Walrus. Then the crones began listing all of the many things they wanted; things they would cross oceans to get.

"We want the diamonds!"

"And the æther!"

"I want my hand back!"

"I want to turn *him* into a pot of tea!"

"But more than all that, we want the *snow!*"

"And we want it *now!*"

Lettie ignored them. She held her handful of pepper dust.

Lettie Peppercorn, get a move on. It's now or nevermore for you.

Raising her hand to her nose, she sniffed it all up.

For a second, Lettie hung just above the water. In her head the pepper itched and burned. She took in a great gasp of air, and:

"Aaaaaaaaaaa-CHOO! Aaa-CHOO! Aaa-CHOO!"

Out came the three biggest sneezes of her life. The force of each one made her stumble backward.

She opened her eyes and wiped away frozen tears. Had her plan worked?

"Yes!" she cheered, doing a little victory skip-and-a-hop on the ocean.

The sea around the *Bloodbucket* had completely frozen. Lettie's subzero sneezes had shot out of her nose and made a whole *iceberg*. Now the whaling ship was utterly trapped inside it. The Walrus's wig had been blown from her head and the Goggler's scopical glasses lay skewed across her face. They blinked, stunned. The *Bloodbucket* had keeled over to one side, encased in the block of ice that nearly reached up to the deck.

"Reverse the engines!" Captain McNulty bellowed. "Reverse!"

The funnels belched smoke, the propellers squealed, the ice boomed and cracked, but the *Bloodbucket* was completely stuck.

Lettie laughed. It had worked. The whalers would have to chip themselves out of the iceberg with harpoons. It would be days before they'd be free to chase *Leutha's Wood*. Now she could head back to Noah and a huge, steaming cup of khave.

She turned and began to skip lightly over the ocean, toward the little wooden ship in the distance.

6

Noah Grows a Blazing Pip

Three things put Lettie in a bad mood on the way back to *Leutha's Wood*.

One: Noah wasn't there to clap and cheer.

Two: He wasn't there to help her out of the sea, either.

Three: Blüstav didn't even say "thank you."

Lettie Peppercorn, why did you bother?

She clambered onto the boat all by herself, stomping over the deck, pulling her feet from her frostprints all the way.

"Get me a hot-water bottle, a blanket, and a cup of tea!" she shouted, barging open the door of the tiny cabin.

"It's nearly done," said Noah at his stove, boiling up a pan of water.

Lettie felt the air around her crackle. "Well, I want it *now!*"

Noah's stalk shed a leaf as he looked at the floor. She instantly felt terrible for losing her temper. She turned away, biting her lip until she could feel it.

"Sorry, Noah. I sounded just like the Walrus then. I don't mean to be in a grump. It's this æther, it's this stupid *cold.*"

He shrugged and stoked the stove. "I know. It doesn't matter, Lettie. You were stupendous out there. You were a hero."

Lettie felt even more awful after he said that, but a little warmer too, knowing that she had just saved Noah. Now he was there to save her. He motioned her into a chair in the corner, where she sat and waited, watching.

It was a dark little room, full of cozy shadows and comfy smells. Under the scent of candle wax there were other aromas: sawdust, smoke, and cinnamon spice. A shelf was piled with pots, forks, wooden cups, and, of course, her beer-bottle da. The small stove Noah stood over was in one corner, beside a bucket full of dirty dishes. On the far side was an unmade bunk bed; on the wall above the pillow were strange words and symbols drawn in chalk that Lettie decided might be Noah's dream-spells or prayers.

By her chair was a low table, strewn with maps of constellations Lettie had never seen before, as well as strange coastlines with routes and crosses drawn over them in orange and green ink. A plant, hanging in a canvas basket, was humming softly to itself above the porthole window. Lettie studied it for a while, watching as the Wind blew down through the cylindrical leaves, making them sing.

"It's a sing-song shrub," Noah explained when he saw her staring. "I brought it with me when I left home."

She imagined him living here in this room. It was easy. Everywhere there were little touches showing his kindness and caring—things she knew already. But the cabin also revealed things she didn't know: how messy he was, and how lonely. She thought of him afloat and alone on the wide, wide sea, with no family or friends. How he must miss his home. Why else would he bring a singing plant from the fifth continent? Lullabies at bedtime, of course.

"Right," said Noah, snapping her from her

thoughts. "Water's boiled. You'll be all defrosted in no time."

He fetched a blanket, a hot-water bottle, and a thermometer. He draped the blanket around her, but it went stiff and shattered. The hot-water bottle froze as soon as he put it by her feet. He stuck the thermometer under her tongue, but the red bar wouldn't even budge past the lowest temperature (which was -50°). Lettie groaned and spat it onto the floor.

"Nothing's helping!"

"I'll boil some more water," said Noah. "You just worry about getting warm."

"I *am* worrying about getting warm!" she snapped. "Sorry. I just did it again."

Noah shrugged and his stalk shook as his shoulders came down. "Guests are allowed to be grumpy."

"Only the ones who have paid," she mumbled. "I'm not meaning to be nasty, Noah. I'm just scared."

There was a little silence. Even the Wind was still.

"Four drops is a lot of æther," he said quietly.

"Oh, Noah," said Lettie. She fought back tears, because they would only freeze in her eyes. "I don't think I can stand it! I might stay cold like this for months, or years."

"I don't think so," said Noah. "Because I make very good soup."

"What should I do?" asked Lettie.

"Wait there," said Noah. "And try not to sneeze."

Then he chopped two onions (diced), three garlic cloves (sliced), and a sweet potato (grated).

Lettie watched:

"Bring it to the boil slowly, Noah."

"That's a lot of garlic, Noah."

"Don't grate your thumb."

Noah grew some peas and split the pods over the pan. He stepped back from the stove, leaving the soup to simmer.

"Just one more thing to add, to make it spicy," he said, wiping his brow on the back of his hand.

"Pepper?" suggested Lettie.

"Something more special than that."

"Oh." Lettie frowned. "What then? Not ginger. I *hate* ginger."

Noah clenched his fists and screwed his eyes shut. Blood rushed to his face and his forehead shone with sweat. He shook, he gasped for breath.

A green stem grew from his stalk, and on the end of the green stem hung a tiny, flame-red chili.

He picked it and held it gingerly, as if at any moment it might burst into flames. "A Blazing Pip, it's called. The hottest thing I can grow. Let me ladle up a bowl for myself first. Then I'll add the Pip . . . and you can eat. You must be hungry."

"I'm nothing but cold, cold, cold." She sat in the chair, feeling like a grandma.

"You won't be cold much longer." Noah crushed the Blazing Pip and Lettie felt a ripple of heat through the air that made her eyes prickle. He dropped it in her bowl, and brought it over with a spoon to where Lettie sat.

"Eat it quick as you can," he said. "While it's hot."

"I'll sip slowly, Noah. It's good manners not to slurp." She brought the soup to her lips and took a sip.

"Feel anything?"

"Just cold."

Noah looked nervous. "Try gulping."

Lettie slurped a bit more, and now she could feel something tingling on her tongue, like tiny bubbles. She took another spoonful, and the bubbles started in her stomach too. "What's happening?" she cried anxiously.

Noah smiled back. "It's working."

Lettie's face began to soften slowly, slowly, into a huge smile. "I can feel it, Noah! My stomach is warm, oh! I can't tell you how wonderful it feels. Tingly and crackly!"

She dropped the spoon, tipped back the bowl, and slurped the rest of the soup down.

"Who cares about good manners!" she said, thrusting the bowl into his hands and letting out a gigantic burp, low and long as a ship's horn.

"Lettie!" said Noah, mouth open. "You're defrosting!"

She laughed out loud—even if she was a little embarrassed—and white steam flew from her lips.

"I can feel it," said Lettie, putting her hands up to her face. "Oh, I can feel my cheeks again! Thank you, Noah! That soup was really, really hot."

"It's my specialty," he said proudly.

"It's boiling and bubbling. I think it's spreading down my arms! And there's something building up in my head too . . ."

Just then she heard a high hissing noise.

"Is that more steam?" she said as Noah began to laugh.

"That's right," Noah told her. "It's coming out your ears . . . Now it's coming out your nose!"

Lettie could barely hear him above the hissing that had now risen to a whistling. "I'm glad you're laughing!" she shouted, putting on a pretend frown. "My head's a kettle!"

She'd spent a whole morning without any warmth, and now she was piping hot. It was a wonderful feeling.

"Let's just hope you come off the boil soon," said Noah, a touch of worry in his voice.

But Lettie could already hear the whistling fade, and as it did she was reunited with her whole face again: eyes, ears, mouth, and nose. All her old friends. It was good to have them back.

"Oh, I need a handkerchief," she said, her eyes and nose streaming. "Everything's runny! Quick!"

She wiped away her tears and blew her nose hard on a leaf that Noah yanked from his stalk. They were tears of happiness at being safe and alive. She was warm right down to her toes, and utterly exhausted. She couldn't help but close her eyes. Noah's smile was like the crescent moon. The sing-song shrub hummed a lullaby.

"How do you feel?" asked Noah.

"Tired."

He asked her a hundred other questions—about what the crones had said, about how she had come up with the plan—but that was the only one Lettie remembered answering.

Where the Wind Blows

Lettie woke to the salty smell of more soup on the stove. She sat up and groaned. "What time is it?"

"Late enough for supper," Noah said. "You slept for the whole day."

Lettie looked through the porthole, at the darkness.

"Is Blüstav still out there?" she asked.

"Course he is. I had to give him a gas lantern, though. He says he doesn't like the dark."

"Serves him right for everything," said Lettie, and flopped back in her chair.

"How do you feel?"

"Like one big bruise."

"Eat," he commanded, handing her a bowl of broth and gray shells.

"Only if you tell me what it is."

"Clam soup," he said proudly. "Another of my specialties. Even Blüstav enjoyed it!"

"Blüstav." Lettie scowled at the mention of him. "You fed him too, did you?"

"I had to," chuckled Noah. "He can't feed himself with that cloud under his coat. He spilled most of the soup, but he managed a clam or two."

Lettie looked down at her bowl. The clams didn't *look* very tasty, but it would be rude not to try. She scooped one from its shell and chewed. It was hot, salty, and delicious. She sipped the broth and sighed with happiness.

"Thank you, Noah. They're delicious."

He laughed. "All part of the service!"

She laughed too. "You shouldn't have let me sleep so long, though!"

"I couldn't wake you," said Noah. "You were dreaming deep, saying things."

"Was I?" Lettie felt herself turn red. "What things?"

"Mostly mumbles," said Noah, going over to his desk and sifting through the maps. "Then you started talking about your ma."

"Oh," said Lettie. "So it was a good dream." She cursed herself for not being able to remember it.

"You said, 'The first rule of alchemy is: Things change,'" Noah told her. "Here it is!" He found the star map he wanted and rolled it up.

Lettie nodded. "That sounds like something my ma would say to me. I suppose it's true. But can things ever change back, Noah?"

"Course they can!" he said, stopping to look at her. "You took æther; you were colder than anyone's ever been before. But now you're fine again."

"Thanks to you."

"What else do you want to change back, Lettie?"

She took a deep breath, because what she wanted to say next could only be said in the simplest of words and she had to make sure that Noah understood them.

"I just want to see Ma, and for it not to be a dream."

Noah nodded and waited for her to carry on.

"I want to see the inn and Da back to normal too, but I'm at sea now and everything seems so far away."

"I know."

"Will I ever see the inn again?"

His eyes shone. "Yes."

"What about Da? Will I ever see him back to normal?"

"Yes."

"And what about Ma?"

"Yes, Lettie. You'll see her."

Lettie smiled. Somehow, Noah saying it made her sure that it would happen. Then she bit her lip. "But when? Where?"

Noah took a gas lantern, stuck the map under his arm, and shrugged on his coat. "Where the Wind blows, of course."

"What does that mean?"

"That's where we'll find her. Wherever the Wind takes us to, that's where she'll be."

"But . . ." Lettie threw her hands in the air, struggling with the strangeness of it all. "Noah, we're wandering off into the ocean, led by a breeze!"

"What's so odd about that? When you're sailing the sea, that's all you can do. If the Wind wants us to travel this way, then we will."

He took her bowl and put it in the bucket with the others. "I'm going outside, to see if I can work out which direction we're headed."

"What should I do?" said Lettie.

Noah shrugged. "Relax."

The cabin door creaked open and shut, and she was alone.

"I'll tidy up," said Lettie, looking around. "This place is a mess."

But before she started on the cabin, Lettie had to tidy up herself. She was a mess too. She took off her shoes and socks for the first time since leaving Barter. Somehow, the muck and grit of the town had got into her shoes, and now her feet were filthy.

She went to the water bucket, wet a cloth, and scrubbed them hard. Nothing happened. Her feet stayed speckled with gray.

Worry crept up on her. She scrubbed them again. Again.

"What's happened?" Saying the question aloud scared her even more.

Perhaps she should use soap. Maybe the grit and grime was just caked on. Perhaps she was just imagining things.

"No, I'm not," she said to herself. She wasn't imagining, she was *petrifying*! Her feet weren't dirty; they were turning to stone, just like Periwinkle. Pulling on her socks and shoes, quick as she could, she sat on the bed breathing hard.

"I should never have left the inn," she whispered. "I shouldn't have done it!"

There was *something* in the ground that Ma had warned about in her note. It was real. And Lettie hadn't listened, and now this . . .

Lettie Peppercorn, you think about something else.

But she couldn't. Whatever was happening scared her, and there was not a lot of good being scared when she was on a tiny wooden boat in the middle of the sea, miles from home.

She willed herself to be calm. Last night her feet had petrified, but now she was miles away from Barter, so it couldn't happen anymore. She was safe.

Wasn't she?

"Lettie Peppercorn!" she hissed. "Stop worrying and do something *useful*."

So she did the washing up. It helped to take her mind off her feet, at least. Scrubbing the dirty bowls, Lettie's thoughts returned to Periwinkle, and she realized how much she missed him. She'd got so much to tell him about: snow, her trip across the sea, and her new friend Noah. She ended up talking to Da instead, still on the shelf above the stove.

"Noah's messy like you, Da. Just look. But he does make very good soup."

Lettie looked up at Da, and thought of him back on the jetty. She'd assumed he was just babbling nonsense, but maybe there had been some sense in him that night.

"I'm sorry I broke my promise to you, Da. Is this what touching the ground does to me?"

Da just sat on his shelf, being a bottle.

"Well," she said. "I hope you're happy. I can look all the way to the horizon now and there's no ground in sight."

She stacked the plates, made the bed, and watered the sing-song shrub. After that she paced about, still feeling restless. Lettie was not used to being a guest. She wasn't sure she liked it. She was only a guest because of Noah: on *Leutha's Wood*, he was in charge. He knew how to steer and how to tie complicated knots and rig sails. Lettie realized with sudden shock that she hadn't any jobs left. She decided at once that she would march outside to Noah and *demand* to be given one.

But then she stopped.

Lettie Peppercorn, what on earth are you doing?

This was the first time in her life that she didn't have to look after anyone but herself! No guests to serve! No Da to scold! No Peri to feed!

She felt lighter. She felt excited. She was on an adventure, and she felt twelve years old not twelve hundred, for once.

"What shall I do with myself?" said Lettie. "I'll go and look at the stars, that's what!"

But before she did, she whispered to Da that even though she was stonesick and homesick, anxious and scared, there was something else that shone through all the bad feelings. She was happy.

Outside, the night was very cold and clear as glass.

"I love the stars," said Lettie, looking up. She felt herself swaying along with the ship. "You can look up at them and forget everything else."

Noah was looking at the stars too. His constellation maps were spread across the deck and he had fastened them to the wood with thorns from his stalk.

"That's what snow reminded me of, when I first saw it," said Blüstav's disembodied voice from somewhere above them. "Stars."

"No, it didn't," snapped Lettie. "It made you think of diamonds, and getting rich. Why are you such a liar?"

"I'm not," Blüstav lied.

There was something troubling Lettie. It was her nose. She could smell a saltiness in the air that set her on edge. What was it?

"I've something to tell you," said Blüstav.

"Be quiet," said Lettie, trying to concentrate on her nose. "I'm ignoring you."

"Then you're a fool, because it's important."

"Can you smell something?" she asked Noah, but he was immersed in his maps.

"I've just worked out our longitude," he announced.

Lettie sniffed the salty smell again. It was still there, and getting stronger. It had a metallic tang that she could almost taste. She felt queasy. And why was she suddenly scared?

"What *is* that?" she said to herself.

"We're north . . . " answered Noah. "*Way* north."

"We're in whaling territory," called Blüstav. "I said *whaling territory*."

And Lettie realized what the smell was: blood.

It was the *Bloodbucket*!

"They're out there!" she shouted to Noah. "I know it! There's blood and coal in the air. It's the crones!"

"Are you sure?" Noah frowned. "It should've taken the *Bloodbucket* days to dig out of all that ice."

"I think you underestimate their industriousness," said Blüstav cheerfully. "If I were you, I'd let me down. Only my alchemy can defend you."

Lettie felt her insides twisting. Blüstav's voice had a gloating edge. Something wasn't right here.

"He's up to something," she murmured. If only she could look at him she might be able to figure out what, but all she could see of the alchemist was a little glow, high up in the blackness.

"He's trying to scare us," said Noah. "We're safe for now. They won't find us in the dark."

"Not unless they had a light to follow," said Blüstav, holding his lantern high.

Something came out of the darkness toward them like a falling star.

THWUNK!

It hit the mast, embedding itself in the wood just above the sail—a harpoon with a rag of burning pitch wrapped around the shaft.

Lettie couldn't move; she was hypnotized by the flames, paralyzed by terror. What should she do? Pull out the harpoon? Put out the flames?

"Time to let me down now!" sang Blüstav.

Then the sail caught fire. In seconds it was ablaze, and the deck filled with smoke, sparks, and the smell of burning. A second harpoon hit the cabin door. Noah yanked it from the wood and tossed it into the sea.

"We've got to get away!" Lettie shouted to Noah.

"How can we?" he called back. "We don't have a sail!"

The Ship Sinks

Lettie was panicking. With no sail, they were dead in the water, and they were running out of options. Was lying, thieving Blüstav their only hope?

What about the æther?

She pulled the bottle from her apron and shook it. Nearly empty. She unscrewed the pipette and held it to the light of the burning deck. Three drops left. Three drops weren't enough: she needed four and a peppercorn if she was to freeze the whaling ship again. It was hopeless anyway—how could she sneeze on the *Bloodbucket* when she didn't even know where it was?

"I've been in this situation before," Blüstav called. "I

With a dreadful, drowning feeling, Lettie realized the Wind could no longer help them. They had no sail. They were on their own.

She searched frantically for the *Bloodbucket*. Somewhere out in that blackness, it lurked. Somewhere out in that blackness, the old crones watched them burn.

"They've snuck up on us, Lettie. They must have put out all their lights and engines, that's why we can't see or hear them."

Lettie looked up at Blüstav, floating above the deck with his lamp shining in the night.

"You led them right to us!" she shouted. "Why would you do that?"

"Because you have to let me down now," laughed Blüstav. "You need my help. You need my alchemy."

have other alchemicals, apart from æther, and I know how to use them to escape. Pull me down, girl!"

THWUNK! Another harpoon hit, starting another fire. Noah was still struggling to put out the other two.

"Do it, Lettie!" he cried.

Gritting her teeth, swallowing her anger, Lettie began to haul Blüstav down to the deck. He came from out of the night sky, plucking alchemical bottles from his pockets. Most of his icicle beard had drizzled away, and his hair was plastered all over his forehead. Now the æther had drained out of him, he looked older. His eyes were light brown, and slyer than ever.

"Tie the rope so I can float just above the deck," he ordered.

Muttering curses under her breath, Lettie obeyed.

"First, we need something to help put out those fires," said Blüstav, clearly enjoying himself. His voice crackled and boomed like it did when he sold the snow.

He handed Lettie bottle after bottle. There were six of them in all, and she looked at them with utter bewilderment. There were powders, liquids—even an aerosol with a vaporizer nozzle at the end. There were bottles in blue, green, and gray; in the shape of spheres, cubes, and pyramids. But Lettie didn't have time to experiment. She needed to know what to do *now*.

"You'll have to mix them all up," he said.

"What? But I'm not an alchemist, Blüstav!"

"Don't panic, girl. I shall instruct you!"

"But we don't have *time*!"

And then, Lettie felt the hand of the Wind. It just fell into hers and tugged her toward the mast. Lettie ran there so quick she nearly flew.

"Come back!" called Blüstav. "I haven't said anything yet!"

Lettie ignored him. She didn't see how the Wind could know alchemy, but she trusted it more than she trusted Blüstav.

"Help me," she said to the Wind, closing her eyes.

And through Lettie, the Wind began to work.

Her hands moved as if they belonged to somebody else. They sprayed, smeared, and shook alchemicals over the mast. Then the Wind finished its alchemy, Lettie's hands dropped to her sides and she stood back to watch.

The wood of the mast began to bubble and bend. It creaked and groaned as it came to life.

Noah looked over to her desperately, his face black with soot. "I need an extra hand here!"

"I think that's what I'm giving you, Noah!"

Two joints appeared: at the elbow and wrist, and

the top of the mast split into five fingers. The wooden mast arm flexed its muscles and ripped off the burning sail, throwing it like a rag to the ocean.

"I've just turned the mast into an arm!" cried Lettie.

Creaking and groaning, the mast-arm bent over into the sea. With a cupped hand, it scooped a hundred bucketfuls of water and sloshed them all over the deck. Lettie and Noah were instantly drenched, but so were the fires.

Lettie wiped sea water from her eyes and shouted for joy. The fires were out! She was filled with the wonder that this was *her* alchemy, and it was *actually working*.

The crones on the *Bloodbucket* had to be watching everything, because now another harpoon fired into the mast-arm, just below the bicep. It made rude gestures into the night.

"How did you . . . ?" began Blüstav, but he was so flabbergasted he couldn't finish.

Lettie felt the Wind again take hold of her. She let it lead her to one side of the ship, then the other, where she sprinkled the wood with alchemicals.

"What are you *doing*?" cried Blüstav.

"I don't know!" said Lettie, eyes closed. "Trusting the Wind."

On either side of the ship, the wood began to ripple and swell. Feathers sprouted from the planks! A great pair of white wings unfolded from port and starboard, stretching themselves out and beating the air with massive strokes.

Leutha's Wood sped through the water, almost sweeping Lettie off her feet. She let out a cheer as the Wind roared past.

"They should have known better than to pick a fight with a master alchemist like me!" Blüstav gloated.

Lettie scowled. It was just like him to take all the credit.

Faster and faster the boat's wings flapped, a thousand times bigger and whiter than a swan's. *Leutha's Wood* shuddered, groaned, and began to lift clear of the water. The mast-arm turned back and waved good-bye in the direction of the *Bloodbucket*. Lettie felt the ship lurch as it rose into the air.

"Up, up, up!" Lettie cried. "Come on!"

"I have to say, this will go down as one of my easiest escapes ever," boasted Blüstav's voice over the sound of beating wings.

But then a well-aimed harpoon shot through the air, pinning one of the wings to the hull, and *Leutha's Wood* plunged back into the sea.

Lettie stumbled into a tangle of old nets as freezing water swelled and swept over her. She staggered to her feet, coughing and shivering. The broken wing twitched feebly. White feathers smoldered to black, then burst into flames.

"I *told* you to follow my instructions!" shouted Blüstav. "This is all your fault!"

"What else can I do?" Lettie whispered to the Wind. "Help!"

But the Wind had fallen silent. It was out of ideas.

Lettie looked to Noah as feathers and harpoons fell like rain around them, and fresh fires burned. *Leutha's Wood* was being eaten alive by flames.

"Noah," she said. "Your boat . . . I'm sorry."

He wiped something from his eye, shrugged, and said nothing.

"What do we do?" said Lettie.

As the fires blazed, they lit up the sea, and Lettie and Noah could finally see the *Bloodbucket*, a hundred yards away. As they watched, its engines sputtered to life and it began to move toward them.

Lettie gulped, reaching for Noah. Just half an hour before she had felt safe and free. Now this. Now the adventure was to end like this.

Leutha's Wood groaned like it was dying and began

to pitch into the sea. Noah wept softly next to Lettie, and never in her life had she felt so terrible, because she knew that to him this ship was his freedom, home, and ancestor. She felt all this was her fault.

The *Bloodbucket* drew alongside them. From above, whalers threw down harpoons with ropes attached. They clambered onto *Leutha's Wood*. There was Grot-Nose Charlie, with his weeping nostrils and a dagger between his teeth. There were the Creechy twins, each with a cutlass, a flaming torch, and seven fingers between them. There was the Goggler, her silver pistol tucked into her skirt. Finally, there was the Walrus, slopping tea everywhere and holding on to a bazooka—a huge blunderbuss rifle from the Orient that fired tiny sticks of dynamite.

"Here's something Captain McNulty had hanging in his cabin," said the Walrus, patting the bazooka fondly. "Without it, we might still be trapped in that iceberg of yours."

"It was more a snot-berg," said Lettie, and the Walrus scowled.

"I believe you have something that belongs to us!" she snapped.

The Goggler's eyes flicked around the deck and spied the empty suitcase. "Where is it?"

"Help!" cried Blüstav, tugging at the knot tethering him to the ship.

The Goggler's beady eyes fixed on him. "Ah," she said, with a wicked grin. "There it is."

The Creechy twins sniggered and one of them scratched a *C* into the decking.

Noah narrowed his eyes. "Don't you graffiti my grandma," he warned, but they ignored him.

"Will ye be wantin' us to pry it out of him, miss?" the twins asked the Goggler in unison.

Blüstav whimpered, and Lettie felt suddenly fierce. Her old landlady instinct came back: *I am in charge and it's up to me to sort it all out.*

"You leave him alone!" she shouted. "What's he done to you?"

"I beg your pardon?" cried the Walrus, steam rising from under her wig. She hooked her finger round the bazooka's trigger and pointed it at Blüstav, who cringed in terror. "This man turned my head into a pot of *tea!*"

The Goggler turned to the whalers. "Get us that cloud from under his coat, you miserable sea vermin, and we'll fill up your hold with diamonds."

The Creechy twins laughed and Grot-Nose Charlie grinned.

"Don't you dare!" said Lettie in a panic. "This is against the law! And no one's above the law!"

One of the Creechy twins stopped and put his cutlass to his lip in an expression of deep thought. "That be true," he said.

"But then," said his brother, "the law belongs to Barter, not to the sea."

And they both leaped forward.

Lettie shut her eyes and screamed, and the Creechy twins screamed too.

That's strange, she thought, opening her eyes.

One of the Creechy twins was gone: vanished. His brother was pointing at the mast-arm.

"Man overboard!" he yelled.

They all looked up at the mast-arm, just as it reached down and flicked the second Creechy twin off the deck as if he were something disgusting, like a booger. He flew into the air and, with a shout and a scream and a splash, he was gone.

"God's beard!" said Grot-Nose Charlie. He yelled up to the *Bloodbucket*. "Get the crane! Get the crane!"

The mast-arm balled into a fist and tried to splat Grot-Nose Charlie on the deck, but he jumped aside, stabbing with his dagger.

The Goggler stomped her feet and fired her pistol, but the tiny bullet couldn't hurt the mast-arm. It tried squashing her underneath its thumb, but nimble as a flea, the Goggler jumped backward. "Shoot!" she roared. "SHOOT!"

The Walrus aimed the bazooka and fired. A miniature dynamite stick flew through the air. The mast-arm caught it and tossed it back. It landed a meter or so from the Goggler, its tiny fuse sizzling down to nothing.

"Idiot!" she shrieked at the Walrus. "Foo—"

BOOM!

The blast formed a huge crater in the deck, catapulting the Goggler toward the rail. She rolled under it, clean off the ship, and splashed into the water.

"Granny overboard!" bellowed Grot-Nose Charlie, as the Walrus tried to help the drowning jeweler out.

Blubber Johnson lowered the crane, swung it around, and began to grapple with the mast-arm.

"GET THE ALCHEMIST!" raged the Goggler as the Walrus fished her from the sea. "I WILL DIP HIS FINGERS IN ÆTHER AND SMASH THEM!"

With sounds of splintering wood and screaming metal, the crane tore the mast-arm in two, and it fell, burning, across the deck, separating Lettie, Noah, and Blüstav from the old crones. *Leutha's Wood* might sink at any second.

The Walrus motioned to the crane, and Blubber Johnson came and plucked her and the Goggler from the sinking ship, back to the safety of the *Bloodbucket*.

"We need to go," said Lettie. *"Now."*

Noah just stood numbly, fires burning in his eyes.

"Noah," Lettie said, gently as she could. "Time to abandon ship."

He nodded, blinking back tears and blowing his nose on a leaf.

Lettie brought out the pipette of æther, and with the last three drops she froze the water around *Leutha's Wood* into a patch of ice, big enough for them both to stand on. They dragged Blüstav and his suitcase onto their frozen lifeboat and pushed themselves out to sea.

"Wait!" Lettie cried in horror. "Da! I've forgotten about Da!"

She jumped back aboard *Leutha's Wood* and bundled into the cabin. It was full of smoke and icy water. She waded through, searching for Da. She'd never forgive herself if he sank to the bottom of the sea, never ever ever.

There he was! Still on the shelf above the stove.

Lettie cradled him in her arms. Her feet were numb from cold and her eyes prickled with smoke as she turned and burst outside, and threw herself back on the ice raft.

When the little wooden ship sank forever, Noah choked out an agonized sob, as if part of his heart had just been drowned. His stalk grew a tiny weeping willow and he sat looking out at the dark. All that was left to light the night were burning pieces of wreckage that flickered and rose and fell on the waves like will-o'-the-wisp.

What now? thought Lettie.

What now?

A Little Imagination Is Required

An old length of rope and a suitcase with holes: that was all that was left on the little raft of ice. Somehow, from those things, Lettie had to shape an escape plan, and shape one quickly: she had only minutes before the *Bloodbucket* spotted them.

"Any ideas?" she asked, to no one in particular.

"We're doomed!" wailed Blüstav. "We're dead in the water!"

Lettie looked to Noah, but he just sat huddled up on the ice, hugging his knees. He had not said a word or grown a leaf since *Leutha's Wood* had sunk. Lettie was desperately worried about him. She wanted to cheer him up, somehow. If only she could grow things from a stalk, like he could. When she had been frozen, he had made Blazing Pip soup. What did she have to cheer him up?

An old length of rope and a suitcase with holes.

Sliding over the ice, she sat down next to him. Gentle waves lapped against the sides of the ice raft. Far away, the sun was rising.

"Noah."

His eyes closed.

"I know *Leutha's Wood* meant so much to you. I know she reminded you of your home and your family."

He sniffed and nodded.

Lettie looked down at the waves by her feet. "You must miss home more than ever now."

"Yes," said Noah. "But I love the sea too much."

"I don't know why. I look at it and I just feel cold."

"You can feel the Wind, though. That's what the sea is: freedom. A million invisible roads to everywhere. Before I get planted in the ground and turn into a tree like my grandmother, I want to see the world. And the sea is the only place I know where you can't put down roots."

Lettie smiled. At least she'd got him talking. "But it must be lonely, always traveling."

"The only thing lonelier than traveling," said Noah, "is standing still."

Lettie pondered on that for a long time. "I think," she said slowly, "that before you came, I'd spent my whole life standing still. In a way, I mean. I didn't go into Barter, I didn't have adventures, I didn't laugh much, or imagine much, or hope much. I was stuck in my inn, trying to keep my Da"—she touched the glass beer bottle in her pocket—"out of trouble. And I'm sorry about your boat, Noah, I really am. But I'm not sorry about anything else that's happened, because you're my best friend now, and I'm not standing still anymore." She brushed strands of hair from her face. "I'm *moving*."

Noah didn't look up. For a moment, Lettie thought her words had been useless, but then she looked at his stalk and saw that his weeping willow was starting to blossom.

"Are you all right now, Noah?"

He shrugged and nodded at the same time. Lettie felt happy, cheering him up. That was what best friends were for.

"I'm cold," he said suddenly.

"Me too." She shivered and burrowed her chattering chin into her coat. "Now a little fire wouldn't be so bad."

Noah smiled a bit and turned his green eyes toward her. "What are you thinking, Lettie?"

"I'm thinking two things," she said. "Number one is that we can't stay on this raft."

"Yes."

"And number two is that the Wind is being very mysterious indeed."

"Yes."

"It knows alchemy, Noah. It helped me on the ship. I made an arm and a pair of white wings. But that's impossible."

"It's not impossible," he answered. "Not if the Wind's being controlled by an alchemist."

Lettie got goose bumps at the thought. "You don't mean Ma?"

"Why not?" Noah shrugged. "It would make sense. Maybe she's controlling it, from wherever she is. Helping you to find her."

"Oh, Noah," said Lettie. "If you're right, then Ma never left. She's always been there with me, every day."

"And if I'm right," said Noah, "then following where the Wind blows is leading us to her."

Lettie tilted her head this way and that, as if her head were a cauldron and Noah's idea had to slosh around inside it for a while before it made sense.

"It might," she said eventually, heart swelling.

"It *has* to," said Noah. "There must be some con-nection between your mother's disappearance and the Albion Wind . . ."

"Noah, you're brilliant!" Lettie exclaimed. "You're an utter genius! Now I know what we have to do!"

Blüstav, who had stopped his whining to eavesdrop, said: "What's that?"

"Find a way to follow where the Wind blows!"

"How?" said Noah. "Using an old length of rope and a suitcase full of holes?"

"No," said Lettie. "Using something else."

"Impossible!" called Blüstav. "There's nothing here!"

"There is," said Lettie. "With a little imagination. Noah, can you grow vines? Really strong vines?"

"I don't know," he admitted. "I've never tried before."

"Try now," said Lettie.

After a few minutes, Noah's brow was knotted with effort, and vines were tumbling down his shoulder in thick coils.

"Make them as long as you can," said Lettie.

"What are we using them for?" Noah asked.

"We're going to make a balloon," said Lettie.

Blüstav laughed above them. "I'm sorry to tell you

this, but you need more than *vines* to make a balloon. You need something that *floats*."

Lettie looked up at him.

At once his laughter died and his face cracked. "No," he said.

"Yes," said Lettie.

"No," said Blüstav again. "No, no, no. I'm not a balloon, I'm a *person!*"

"You float," said Lettie. "That's good enough."

"But I don't like heights!" the alchemist wailed. "Floating ten feet off the ground is terrifying enough."

"Will these do?" said Noah, looking exhausted. Thick green foliage curled around his feet.

Lettie smiled. "Perfect."

"You can't do this!" Blüstav roared.

"Yes, I can," said Lettie.

And she did.

Up and Away

It was a glorious dawn; the sea was golden with the rising sun. Lettie and Noah had worked quickly, and in a matter of minutes the balloon was ready. It was simply a net of vines—a sort of hammock—strung around Blüstav's legs and arms. Onto this, they threw the open, empty suitcase. That was their cockpit. There was no rudder and no ballast, so there was no way of going left or right or up or down. Lettie would trust everything to the Wind.

The Wind, as far as she could tell, was excited and anxious. It kept tugging at her, as if to say *Hurry, hurry, hurry!* Well, they were ready to leave.

Now that it was light, they could see the *Bloodbucket* behind them, coming up fast, engines roaring. It was going to be a close thing, indeed.

"Get in!" said Noah, stepping into the suitcase.

Lettie tested the vines. They were strong. They would hold. The most dangerous thing would be if the Wind grew too excited and blew them out of the hammock by accident. Lettie wound her arms and legs around the vines and held on tight.

"Ready!" she said above the ever-increasing roar of the *Bloodbucket*'s engines.

Noah grew a jagged thorn from his shoulder and began to hack at the lead buckles of the suitcase that kept Blüstav anchored down. One clattered free, and they lurched five feet upward.

"One more to go!" yelled Noah.

"Hurry!" Lettie shouted. The Wind screeched around them so hard it made her ears ache and her teeth rattle. She could see the steam-powered harpoon gun bolted to the *Bloodbucket*'s prow. Blubber Johnson was loading a harpoon, and the Walrus was aiming her bazooka straight at them. But then, at last, Noah pried away the last lead buckle. It fell with a *splash* in the sea, and suddenly they were flying.

Lettie's stomach lurched as they soared into the sky. She looked behind her where the furious faces of the crones grew smaller and smaller.

Above, Blüstav's coat bulged and strained, the snow cloud soared. Lettie wondered what the alchemicals were that made it so much lighter than air. She decided to ask Ma when she finally saw her again.

"We're safe!" said Noah, his leaves turning toward the sun. "And it's good to feel warm again."

They climbed higher and higher. Now the clouds were close enough to touch. Below, the sea was laid out like a very blue tablecloth, constantly wrinkling then smoothing out. Upon it Lettie saw the *Bloodbucket*, tiny as a toy, and the wide, white V it made through the sea as it followed them.

Lettie took out her telescope. Pulling it open, she looked to the deck of the whaling ship and began to giggle. The giggle grew, and before she knew it, Lettie was laughing so hard the suitcase had nearly turned over.

"Careful!" cried Noah.

Lettie fought back the giggles, which nearly overwhelmed her again. She put the telescope down and wiped her eyes.

"Sorry, Noah," she said, gasping for breath. "You'd be laughing too, if you could see them."

"Who?"

"The Goggler and the Walrus. They're on the *Bloodbucket*, looking up at us. They're so furious, the Walrus has torn up her wig again and the Goggler's stomped on her scopical glasses."

Noah giggled. "Now what are they doing?"

Lettie gasped. "They're turning on each other. The Goggler's kicking the Walrus in the shin! Oh, it's vicious! The Walrus is hopping about, eyes popping, chins wobbling. You can see she's not in that much pain, though. She's biding time, coming up with her revenge! The Goggler's turned to storm off."

"I doubt she's going to—" Noah began.

"Wow!" yelled Lettie. "Out shoots the Walrus's hand! I thought she only moved that fast for cakes! She's hoisting the Goggler up by the ankle, the old bag's screaming and struggling to get away, but she's helpless. The Walrus is holding her up over her head, and . . . and . . . and she's dunked the Goggler headfirst!"

Noah grinned. "Into the sea?"

"No, into her own tea-filled head! Like a cookie!"

And together Lettie and Noah laughed and laughed and laughed until they ached with relief. They were free. They were together. They were safe.

When it became clear that the vines were holding, and once the Wind had died down a little, Lettie began to relax. It was peaceful up here. She cradled Da in her arms—she wasn't having him fall from her pocket and into the sea. From this height, his glass would shatter. She felt sick thinking of all the times in the past day where she might have lost him forever. Holding him up to the sun, she looked for any cracks in his glass. There didn't seem to be any.

"I wonder when Da will change back," she said to Noah.

"I should think it will be a while yet," he answered. "He *swallowed* that alchemical. The Walrus and the Goggler only got it on their skin, and they're still changed."

"He looks a little shaken," said Lettie. "He's all fizzed up."

Noah smiled. "I know how he feels. I'm glad he's all right, though."

"I'm glad too," said Lettie fiercely, and she meant

it, which surprised her. "I thought he was nothing but trouble; I was wrong. He's also my da, and that means something. Even if he's a bad da most of the time, it still counts."

"He'll be better when he changes back, Lettie. I know it."

"I know it too!" she said passionately. "He'd *better* be better, for his sake. It's the first rule of alchemy, Noah: things change!"

Noah raised his eyebrows. "You sound angry!"

"Of course I am! Angry at him. And worried, and guilty, and frustrated . . . but I love him too. That more than anything." She cradled Da and said it again, in case he hadn't heard. "More than *anything*."

"I hope he was listening," said Noah, laughing. "Even though he doesn't have ears."

Lettie smiled. Noah was one of the wisest people she'd ever met, but he was forgetting that there are some things you don't need to hear. Some things you just know, and love is one of them.

They rose into the clouds, and for a long time saw nothing but mist. The Wind died down and they drifted for what seemed like hours, faces clammy and clothes damp and chill. Lettie couldn't even see Blüstav above them, although she heard him sneezing.

"I have the most dreadful cold!" he wailed.

"That's what you get after freezing yourself for ten years!" Lettie called back. He wasn't getting *any* sympathy from her.

After that, Blüstav kept a sullen silence.

"Do you think we're almost there?" asked Noah.

"I think so," said Lettie. "Wherever *there* is."

She fizzed with excitement. They were close to Ma, so close. It was another one of those things she just *knew*.

It grew darker all of a sudden, as if they'd passed into shadow. The mist thinned. Lettie held her breath. Something was about to happen.

With a sharp lurch, the balloon stopped moving. Lettie reached into her pocket to clutch Da as they hung suspended.

Blüstav cursed as the nimbostratus rumbled a peal of thunder. "Why have we stopped?" he said. "Have we hit a snag?"

"Yes," said Noah and Lettie together. They were staring at something emerging from the mist like a black bubble.

"What is it?" Blüstav called.

Lettie rubbed her eyes. The vines had caught on a huge iron cauldron, with a pair of bellows underneath for lighting a fire.

"Touch it," whispered Noah. "Make sure it's real."

Slowly, Lettie reached out her fingers, leaning as far as she dared from the canopy, and touched the bellows. They were real. It was all *real*.

Once, Lettie would have exclaimed: "This is impossible!" But the events of the past two days had convinced her that "impossible' no longer existed. She simply didn't believe in it.

Instead, she said: "But what does it mean?"

"What does *what* mean?" Blüstav asked in exasperation.

"Work the bellows," said Noah. "Let's clear this mist and see where we are."

So Lettie began to move the bellows up and down—which was tricky to do without falling out of the hammock—and slowly the room (for it was a room they were in) began to clear.

"But this is impossible!" said Blüstav when he saw where they were.

Lettie looked around in wonder.

They were in a laboratory—a laboratory made

of ice, with tall ceilings and veins of æther running through the walls. There was a tall, open window behind them—it was through there they had drifted.

No wonder it grew darker all of a sudden, Lettie thought. *We went inside!*

The cauldron and the bellows were in the middle of the room, and climbing up each of the four walls were shelves of empty bottles, boxes, and vials. The floor was strewn with old paper and books.

Lettie rolled out of the suitcase and her feet hit the floor. Noah followed. They went to the window and looked through with hearts racing.

Until that moment, ice to Lettie was ugly and treacherous. It froze up windows and stopped her from seeing outside for days at a time. The ice she knew was ugly; muddied brown and gritted gray; sullied with silt, grime, kitchen grease, coal chips, and beer. Never had it occurred to Lettie before that ice might be beautiful.

"Oh," was all she could say.

The laboratory was carved atop a giant iceberg. Below them were wild white crags and the jewel-blue sea. Rising above were shimmering domes with stairways winding up to windowed spires, all of it glinting in the sunlight. Lettie's eyes filled with tears. Not just because the iceberg was the most beautiful thing she'd ever seen, but because she knew that Ma had led her there.

The Wind was all around her, ruffling her hair as if to say: *Look where I brought you! Aren't you pleased?*

"This is my ma's laboratory," whispered Lettie. "The one Blüstav told us about. The place where she made snow."

"It's magnificent!" said Noah with a huge smile, his biggest since *Leutha's Wood* sank. "Whatever the Wind wants you to find, it's here."

Lettie nodded, suddenly nervous. It had been such a long journey: she had traveled by boat, raft, and balloon. She had been colder than she could ever have imagined and seen her da turn into a beer bottle. She had given a ship wings and walked across the waves without sinking. Now she was about to discover the truth about Ma and where she had been all these years, Lettie was sure of it. Soon she would know everything, at long last.

What she wasn't sure of, what she wasn't sure of at all, was whether she was ready for the truth. Maybe it wasn't the truth she wanted. Maybe the

truth was sad or terrible in ways she couldn't possibly imagine.

She turned to Blüstav, snagged on a chandelier.
There were lines on his face that Lettie had never
noticed before. He had been electrocuted so many
times now that all his hair stood on end and little
sparks flew from his mouth as he breathed. He looked
terrified.

"She'll be here," he said with a gulp. "And she won't
be happy with me."

Lettie glanced toward the door, waiting for Ma to
arrive, but her mother appeared exactly the same way
she had disappeared, ten years ago: through the window.

This is how it happened.

A sudden gust of air brought a flurry of clothes
flying in the window. There was a brightly colored
tartan scarf, a leather hat with goggles attached, a
long blue coat buttoned up to the neck, and a pair of
brown Wellington boots. The Wind brought them in
and whirled them around the room, knocking over
armchairs and pots, and tossing old yellow stacks of
paper into the air like confetti. Then the boots landed
on the floor and began hopping to the window, where
Lettie was standing. One boot jumped on top of the
other and kicked it shut. The latch closed with a *click*,

and the Wind ceased. All the clothes fell to the floor in a heap.

Lettie looked on, openmouthed, as the Wellington boots hopped back over to the pile of clothes, which began assembling itself into a person. The boots crawled under the coat, which stood up and put the leather hat with goggles where a head ought to be. The figure wrapped the scarf around its neck and marched over to Lettie, pulling out a pair of patchwork oven gloves from the coat pockets. She—for it was unmistakably a she, despite being completely see-through—plucked two invisible things from Lettie's fingers and dropped them into each oven glove. Then the oven gloves moved, and it was obvious to Lettie that now they had a pair of hands inside them—invisible hands, but hands all the same.

Then the person leaned down to Lettie and gave her a huge, wonderful, overwhelming hug. All of Lettie's sadness and loneliness was squeezed out of her, and she hugged the person back, because it was Ma. She knew it. She just knew.

And it was wonderful.

PART THREE
Inside an Iceberg

"Turn yourselves from dead stones into
living philosopher stones!"

Gerhardt Dorn, *Philosophia Speculativa*

❧ CONTENTS ❧

Ma

The next moments passed in a slow blur, like they do in dreams. Beyond Ma's arms nothing seemed to exist. To Lettie, those arms were the edges of the world.

"Is this real?" she whispered, afraid that it wasn't.

"I'm here," Ma answered. "I'll never leave you again."

"It feels like a dream, though."

Ma let go of Lettie at last. "You're wide awake," she said, giving her daughter a playful pinch on the arm. "See?"

Taking a handful of string from her coat pocket, Ma began to tie up her sleeves and feet, as if she were making herself airtight.

"I always knew you'd come back," said Lettie, trembling. "But why do you look so . . ."

Ma laughed. "Mysterious?"

"Invisible," Lettie admitted. "And strange."

She took a step back. Something was troubling her. "Ma?"

"What?"

"You ought to give me a kiss."

"I ought to," said Ma. "But I can't."

"Why not?" asked Lettie, a lump in her throat.

Ma sighed and finished tying her oven glove at the wrist. "There's a reason, Lettie, but it's wrapped up in a story . . . a story that stretches back thirteen years, to before you were born."

"I already know how you made snow to save me," said Lettie. "And that Blüstav stole it and marooned you here."

"There's more," said Ma. "Blüstav told you *how* it all happened, and I, as the Wind, made him tell it truthfully. Now I'm going to tell you *why*."

"Be quick!" Lettie begged. "Leave out the boring bits."

"I will, Lettie—but not just yet. There's someone I need to deal with first."

Ma raised her head to look at Blüstav. He was trying to swim away from her, through the air, doggy-paddling toward the window.

"*Blüstav, stop!*" commanded Ma. "You stole my snow. *Lettie's* snow."

Lettie had never seen the alchemist so red in the face. His hands groped at the air, like he was searching for an excuse. He blinked and ran a sweaty palm across his forehead.

"I, ah . . . I thought you'd just make some more," he blustered.

"And how could I? You broke all my instruments! Stole my alchemicals! *Trapped* me here! Oh, Blüstav," said Ma sternly. "We really have to do something about that imagination of yours, your lies are so predictable! Stealing snow was your revenge, wasn't it?"

Silence.

"*Wasn't it?*" Ma repeated firmly.

Blüstav nodded and drifted to a stop, a few feet from the window.

"Sorry . . ." he mumbled.

"It's not *me* who has to forgive you," said Ma. "It's Lettie. It's *her* life you put in danger."

Lettie saw now how powerful an alchemist Ma really was: in just a few words, she'd transformed

Blüstav from an arrogant con man into a shy, awkward child. And he actually sounded sorry!

With Blüstav dealt with, Ma turned her attention elsewhere.

"You must be Noah," she declared, marching over to him. She held out an oven glove, and he shook it. "You're the best friend my daughter has ever had, Noah. I should know, because I found you! A boy who follows the wind without asking why, that's who you are. I searched the whole world over for you."

Noah and his flower blushed red as a rose.

Ma laughed. "Now, what shall we do about those old crones? I passed their ship on the way here."

"Are they *still* after us?" said Lettie in dismay. "I thought they were busy fighting each other. Why don't they just give up?"

"Because money makes people mad, Lettie. And the idea of *more* money . . . well that just feeds their insanity. More, more, more. That's all they think of now. Snow has made them *dangerous*."

"Can't you change them into something harmless?" said Lettie. "Like squirrcls?"

"Or cushions?" suggested Noah.

Ma smiled. Lettie could tell because her goggles lifted up.

"It'll take them time to find us," she said. "And even when they do, we'll be safe. The doors to the staircase are still frozen shut, I should think. Let's see if I'm right!"

She ran through the door. Lettie and Noah followed, dragging Blüstav along by the vines that were still wrapped around him. He trailed after them, bumping his head on every door frame and snagging on chandeliers. But he didn't moan once: he was too afraid of Ma.

Lettie ran faster, trying to keep up, but she couldn't help glimpsing into each doorway she rushed past. And there were dozens. One room held a great silver spinning wheel, all bent and twisted. Another room held a collection of glass tubes in the shape of bells, but most of them had been smashed. Then they came to the blue doors encased in ice that Blüstav had frozen shut with æther, years before.

"See?" said Ma. "We're safe."

"You mean *trapped*," muttered Blüstav. "There's no way out."

Ma turned to look at him, and he fell silent.

Lettie didn't care about the doors. She just wanted an explanation. Ma knew it too.

"Come on," she said. "Let's go back to the laboratory, snuggle in those armchairs, and try to forget who might be coming up the stairs. I'll explain, and Blüstav can get the tea."

So the four of them went back to the laboratory, where the armchairs were waiting. Noah grew tea leaves and cinnamon for the cauldron, and Ma lit the tinder underneath. Soon the fire was roasting. After hours up in the freezing clouds, Lettie felt the damp seep out of her at last. She wriggled deep into her armchair and marveled at how the room stayed frozen, despite the fire.

They hadn't any water, so Ma broke a window pane and left the icy shards in the cauldron to melt. Blüstav floated above, stirring with his spoon. Then Lettie dipped the mugs into the cauldron and handed them to Noah and Ma, who didn't drink the tea, but took a straw from her coat to suck up the steam. Noah and Lettie leaned back in the armchairs, and sipped and sighed, and were happy and warm at last, at last.

"Tell it, Ma," said Lettie. "Tell the story of snow."

"It's not snow's story," said Ma. "It's *yours*. But first things first: Where's your da?"

Lettie took Da from her pocket and showed him to Ma.

"Oh, my love," said Ma sadly. "You've really let yourself go. How did that happen?"

"Blüstav did it," said Lettie.

"I'm not talking about that, Lettie. I mean *before* he turned into a beer bottle. How did he get to be so bad at looking after you? He made your life hard. You weren't the landlord's daughter; he was the landlady's father."

"Yes," said Lettie, slipping Da back inside her coat pocket to warm him up again. "I'm his landlady and I'll look after him forever."

"You won't have to," said Ma sternly. "He'll have to change, Lettie. We all will, if we become a family again. Would you like that?"

"More than anything," Lettie answered. "Can it really happen, though?" she added. "We haven't been a family for such a long time."

Ma was silent for a moment.

"You still love your father, don't you?" she asked. "After everything he's done?"

Lettie felt the weight of Da in her pocket and nodded.

"Then it *can* happen," said Ma emphatically. "Becoming a family . . . now that's alchemy beyond what I know. Beyond what *anyone* knows. But I'm sure it starts with love."

Lettie smiled. She was sure of that too.

"But you mustn't think it will be easy, Lettie. Love

makes things possible, not easy." Ma sipped her tea thoughtfully. "Now I'm ready to explain," she said after a time. "I had to wait until you all had your tea, you see; for it's a bitter story, and it's good to have a cup of something sweet in your hand when you hear it."

The Making of
Lettie Peppercorn

The truth is Lettie wasn't born the way other babies are born. She was special; she was different; she came out of a cauldron one Sunday afternoon. Teresa reached in, lifted her out, and there she was—a beautiful baby, made with alchemy and love. She had wide, wonderful eyes. They opened, and looked straight at Teresa, who said:

"Hello, Lettie Peppercorn. I'm your ma."

Before Lettie, Teresa had waited ages for a baby.

"Why is it taking so long?" she asked.

Everyone had a different answer: Doctor Nickles recommended more tests, Reverend Gumpfrey recommended more prayer, and page sixty-four of Sister Mary Bruise's All You Need to Know about Your First Baby *recommended more waiting.*

But Teresa had had enough of waiting. She was desperate. And she said so.

"I've had enough of waiting! I'm desperate! Henry, pass me my cauldron, please!"

"You're going to make a baby using alchemy?" asked Henry.

"Yes, I am."

"Is it even possible?"

Henry was right to wonder. All the other alchemists were only interested in turning lead into gold. None had ever imagined making a child. There was no recipe for such an experiment. Teresa would have to make it up as she went along.

"Of course it's possible. I made Periwinkle from a pebble last spring."

"Yes, but this is different. This is a child."

"You're right, Henry. It is different. You'll have to help too."

Hardest of all was knowing where in the world to start. Teresa and Henry spent long nights discussing all the hundreds of possible materials from which Lettie could be made.

"How about wood?"

"No, wood is too spiteful. It gives you splinters."

"Gold?"

"Don't be silly, Henry. A child made from gold will grow up to be a spoiled brat!"

"Water?"

"We don't want a crybaby. And the sea is always changing, which means she'll be moody. Oh, it seems like whatever we choose is wrong!"

They went through a thousand possibilities, and none of them seemed right. The problem was this: Teresa wanted to create Lettie, not design her. She wanted Lettie to grow up and decide herself just who she was going to be. She had to be free to carve out her own life.

Then one day, Henry read a line aloud from page eighty-one of Sister Mary Bruise's All You Need to Know about Your First Baby*:*

"When a baby is born, its life is a blank slate."

"That's perfect!" Teresa clapped her hands and kissed him.

"A baby made from slate?" said Henry.

"Don't take things so literally, my dear, have a bit of imagination. We'll use a bit of granite, some flint, a bit of beach shingle . . ."

And so it was decided that Teresa and Henry's baby would be made from stone.

Of course, a baby made from stone would have some of its qualities. And, sure enough, when she grew up Lettie proved herself to be dependable, resourceful, stubborn, and patient. But she was also able to sculpt her own destiny, which is the most important thing about being human.

Michelangelo was a sculptor who said once that when he looked at a stone, he saw the sculpture inside it. All he had to do was take away the bits that weren't needed. It was just like that with Lettie. Teresa looked at the stones around Barter and saw a child within them, patiently waiting to be given life.

It may have seemed to Lettie that her ma had never been part of her life. But Teresa was the one who lifted her from the cauldron. She was there when Lettie took her first step, and spoke her first word (it was "Dada," which made Teresa secretly jealous). The three of them lived days of buttered toast and tea, lullabies and bedtime. Teresa was amazed by the alchemy Lettie had brought into the White Horse Inn: Henry had changed into Da, and she had changed into Ma.

But then something happened that made her blood run cold: Periwinkle got sick.

It started when his claws turned gray. Da didn't even notice, but Ma did. She spent every waking moment studying Periwinkle. She counted his heartbeats, measured his breaths and studied his symptoms. She recorded every change in his body as it grew flatter, heavier, grayer. By the end of the week she had come to the inescapable conclusion that her alchemy, no matter how brilliant, was leaking away. Periwinkle was turning back into stone.

But why was he changing?

It took Ma another week of tests and observations before she had the answer: it was Albion. It was the land of slate and cobbles and granite that surrounded Periwinkle. Every slate roof, cobbled street, granite wall, and shingle beach called out, "Change back, change back, change back . . ." It would be a gradual process, but after many years, Periwinkle would turn back into a stone.

And if Periwinkle was petrifying, then that meant Lettie could too.

Ma wrote down her thoughts in a note. She called this one:

WHY PERIWINKLE IS PETRIFYING

Hold two identical glasses in your hands. Fill one with water and leave the other empty. Put a single ice cube in each. Wait, and watch.

What do you see?

Very quickly, the ice cube in the water melts away to nothing.

This demonstrates exactly what is happening to Periwinkle: surrounded by stones, he is slowly disappearing.

From that day forward, stones became Ma's enemy. She searched for ways to get rid of them, to keep them as far from her daughter as possible, before she too began to petrify.

"There has to be a way," said Ma, sitting down to think. "There has to be."

And there was.

It just hadn't been invented yet.

That night Ma packed her suitcase, popped Periwinkle on her shoulder, and climbed from the window of the White Horse Inn, looking for Blüstav. She found him in his laboratory, still sitting in his chair. Almost as if he had never moved.

At the time, she had thought him a little pathetic, to wait for her like a dog. But, of course, he was sitting, patient as a spider; ready to strike, ready to deliver his terrible revenge.

The two of them went out into the ocean, to create a laboratory atop an iceberg. Inside, Ma wrote down the recipe for snow: the invention that would save her daughter's life. Ma's invention was very simple. She designed snow to be a blanket: a blanket to cover up the stony ground. A blanket for Lettie, so that she might be free to walk the earth and never be afraid of petrifying. Ma ordered Blüstav to collect up all the ingredients, then she set to work.

Every day and night for a year Ma worked her alchemy. She spun her silver wheel and she sewed her needle of frost, until the night when snow was finally finished. Ma put down the recipe, looked up at the nimbostratus she had made and smiled: it was done. Now she could leave the iceberg laboratory and take the snow cloud home.

And Ma would have done just that, had she not made one, terrible mistake.

She fell asleep.

When she woke up in the morning, she was filled with horror. Blüstav had stolen snow and escaped. He had broken the silver wheel and smashed the glass bells. He had taken every alchemical and frozen the doors shut with æther. The handle and hinges were blue with ice that would hold for a thousand years. There was no escape, save the window and the sheer drop to the ocean outside.

Thankfully, Blüstav had left the paper and pencils. And so Ma sat down, and ordered her thoughts by jotting them down:

HOW I GET SNOW BACK

1. I need to escape
2. I have to find Blüstav and the snow cloud
3. By the time I get out, he could be anywhere in the world
4. So I have to be quick
5. And I have to be everywhere at once

By the time she had written her third thought, Ma decided the quickest way to find him would be to change herself into air.

Ma, in her laboratory of ice, floating on the waves, wrote her daughter a note. It said:

LETTIE—THESE THINGS YOU MUST REMEMBER:

1. I've gone away to save your life
2. Until I return, you are in danger
3. The danger is inside Albion
4. Don't set a foot upon Albion, for it can kill you
5. I love you, and I'm coming back

She never explained her plan to Da: he would only worry, and try and persuade her to find another way. But there was no other way.

Ma tied the note to Periwinkle and watched him fly off to Barter. Then she turned back to her cauldron and started, once more, to work her alchemy.

She began by skimming æther from overhead storm clouds, using a kite she had made from book pages and string. For a whole day she purified the æther in pots and pans, and distilled it twenty times until it was clear and syrupy, like liquid glass.

On the second day she ripped open her mattress and pillows, for the feathers, and burned them into a powder to dust the æther with. She hoped to capture from the feathers an essence of lightness and gliding. Then she strained the whole thing through a copper gauze. The clear liquid now had a silver sheen. Ma had to weigh her iron cauldron down with bricks—without them it would float fifteen centimeters from the ground. She was pleased.

For all of the third day she let the mixture simmer in the cauldron, while she stirred in a pot of strong glue (Ma wanted her new body to stick together, after all, and air is notoriously slippery) with a silver spatula.

On the fourth day, she added a spurt of steam (for motion), an ounce of quicksilver (for speed) and three sticks of liquorice (for taste, seeing as the mixture had to be swallowed.) She poured it into a tiny vial and stoppered it with a cork. Then she shook it as vigorously as she could and left it on the side to settle.

On the fifth day she rested. And on the sixth day Ma unstoppered the cork, put the vial to her lips, and took the tiniest sip.

The mixture worked.

It was the strangest sensation: similar to what a tree must feel in the autumn when the leaves drift off its branches.

Ma felt bits of her body start to glide out of the laboratory window. Her fingers first, then her toes. She looked down, and they were no longer there. She felt them, though, they were caught by the wind, right this moment they were being tossed around the iceberg by the sea breeze.

Ma held her hand to her face and watched it slowly dissolve. It joined a thermal and rose up through the clouds ... Ma could not even gasp before her lips flew out the window along with her ears, to join an air current heading north.

But as Ma's body turned to air, it did not stick together ... it scattered across the world, taken on the winds. Already her lips and ears were halfway to the Pole, while her fingers were part of a hurricane headed to the East.

The last thing Ma thought before she evaporated completely was that she should have used more glue.

Over the years, while Da grew unlucky and Lettie grew up, Ma flew in one hundred pieces, as part of storms, gales, and breezes, to every corner of the world. And all the while she searched for Blüstav. Her ears listened for him in the many taverns of the world. Her eyes searched for him across oceans and skies. Her fingers felt for him in crowded streets.

She found him wandering the courts of continental kings and queens, selling snowflakes as if they were diamonds. As soon as she caught him, Ma faced another dilemma: now that she was nothing but a breeze, what could she do? What power did she have over Blüstav, who was flesh and blood?

Not much, but a little.

Not much, but enough.

Ma found she could move Blüstav wherever she wanted, like a piece in a chess game.

What, after all, is the wind except for movement? When the wind blows, it says to you, Move with me, move. It is impossible to resist: little by little, it sweeps you along. And that is precisely what happened to Blüstav. He never felt Ma's hands and feet, but every time they swept past him they elbowed, nudged, poked, and kicked him up the bottom, all the way back to Albion. Step by step, without even realizing, Blüstav *headed away from the royal courts, toward Barter.*

Slowly, slowly, slowly . . . Ma led him to the doorstep of the White Horse Inn. It took ten years, but eventually he arrived, asking for a room with a draft.

Ma's plan was simple: she was the Wind, and she was everywhere. Once Blüstav brought the snow cloud back to Lettie, Ma could take hold of her daughter and guide her to the truth.

Of course, things hadn't gone quite as she had intended. Some very nasty old ladies had nearly ruined everything, and slippery Blüstav had nearly gotten away twice. All of which was why Ma had also led a third person toward the White Horse Inn; someone who could help Lettie if she got into trouble; someone who would follow the wind without asking why . . . a green-eyed boy with a stalk on his shoulder.

Yes, it was no coincidence at all that Noah happened to be there the night Lettie's life changed forever. Ma had led him across oceans to the White Horse Inn for one reason only: to be a best friend.

As soon as Blüstav arrived at the inn, Ma began to put herself back together. It was no easy task. She had been tumbling around the world in one hundred pieces for ten years, and she might have done so forever, if it was not for a pair of oven gloves in a Baverian bakery. Her fingers suddenly fell into them as they flew through the town of Blokkenborg.

Suddenly, Ma found she could move them where she wanted. The feeling of freedom was indescribable. Her fingers crawled through the town, with all the market goers screaming and diving behind the baguettes, until they reached a clothes stall. They took a pair of trousers from the rack and dragged them into a nearby forest. Ma knew her legs were about to pass through there, she could feel them. And when they did her fingers held the trousers in just the right place, and in they slipped, a perfect fit.

After that, Ma's legs gave her fingers a lift, and hopped to Venice, where her feet were running through the canals.

The Thief, the Liar, the Cheat, and the Clam

Now Ma had finished her story. The laboratory was still, and the fire dwindled.

Lettie sat and took small, uncertain sips of her tea. It had gone cold, but she barely noticed. She was thinking.

"Are you all right?" Ma said softly.

Lettie wasn't sure yet. She needed to think some more.

"Listening to a long story is like eating too much food," said Ma. "Sometimes you need a bit of time afterward, to sit and digest."

Lettie nodded: she felt *full*, almost to bursting. She

had to get some of her thoughts out before she went *bang*.

"You're made from air," said Lettie.

"Air, æther, and a little glue. Thank goodness you're still only twelve . . . If you were any older you might not have been able to believe it all."

"And I'm . . . I'm made of stone."

"Not just stone," said Ma. "A thousand things besides . . . Alchemy is change, Lettie. And change can't stop. After you were born, we kept adding things into the mix."

"Like what?"

"I don't have the words, Lettie, so I shall have to borrow them from someone else: 'Little, nameless, unremembered acts of kindness and of love,'" she quoted. "That's what we poured into you, after you were born: our love and time and hope. But then I left, and we stopped doing that."

"That's not true, Ma," said Lettie. "When you first came up, you took your hands from me and dropped them into your oven gloves. They've been holding on to me for years, haven't they?"

"That's right," said Ma. "Giving you little tugs in the right direction. They guided you here."

Lettie shook her head in wonder. "I knew there was

something in the wind guiding me, pulling me this way and that. I just never knew that something was *you*."

"It was all the mothering I could do, Lettie, and it wasn't enough, I know. I'm sorry. It took me a long time to put myself back together. But I'm here now, and we can be a family again."

"The strangest family in the whole world," said Lettie. "A stone, a breeze, and a beer bottle."

Ma laughed. "Yes! Though you don't have to worry about being a stone, Lettie. Not now that my old master has come to return what he stole ten years ago."

She looked up to where Blüstav floated, making little whimpering sounds.

"Let it go," Ma said firmly. "It's a cloud, and it belongs in the sky."

"But it's mine," said Blüstav, his voice a squeak. He swam frantically through the air toward the window.

"For ten years, you've put my daughter's life in danger. Now the chase is over. Let it go."

"If you don't, I'll die," said Lettie. "One day, I'll turn to stone. Do you want that to happen?"

He shook his head violently, then yelped as the snow cloud in his coat gave him another shock.

"Where are you going to escape to this time, Blüstav?" Ma asked sternly. "Can you outrun the Wind?"

He reached the window, fumbling at the latch. Watching sadly, Ma stepped on the vines still wrapped around his arms and legs.

"Let me go!" begged Blüstav, throwing open the window.

"You've been freezing cold for ten whole years because of that cloud," said Lettie. "Why don't you just let it go? Please, Blüstav. *Please.*"

There was a tense silence as Blüstav's hand twitched at his collar. He undid a button, slowly, as if it was causing him great agony. A whole minute passed. Another button came loose. A white wisp of cloud slithered out from his neck. He began to sink to the floor.

Lettie was amazed. Finally Blüstav had overcome his greed. He had really *changed*; he'd undergone *alchemy.*

"Thank you," said Ma, holding out her hand for him to shake. "Thank you, Blüstav."

He took her gloved hand, and then Lettie saw that gleam in his eye; that *sharpness.*

"Don't!" she shouted, too late.

Blüstav didn't shake Ma's hand, he pulled. He snatched off her glove and threw it out the window.

"Ma!" Lettie cried.

Ma snatched her sleeve, trying to close the hole, but

already a gust had whipped her from her coat and thrown her around the room. The chandelier rocked, the windows swung, and some old books fell from the shelves. Lettie whirled about, searching for Ma, seeing nothing. Her clothes lay in a heap where she had been. Lifeless things. The oven gloves, the goggles, the blue coat. All tied together with brown string; all empty of Ma.

Where was she? Out the window, above the iceberg, or were parts of her still inside? Lettie's eyes were useless, so she screwed them shut. She *felt* for Ma instead; trying to feel the pull of a hand, but there was no direction to the wind. It pulled and pushed, it nudged left and right, it spun her around. There was no direction. There was no purpose. There was no Ma.

She was gone.

Lettie looked up at Blüstav and shouted, "Why?"

She saw the answer in his eyes, shining like coins. He might have defrosted, but he hadn't changed really. He kicked with his hands and propelled himself outside. Noah leaped for the vines, but they whipped away too fast for his hands, and Blüstav was free.

"That was my ma," Lettie called after him, her voice breaking up into sobs. *"That was my ma!"*

With Noah she ran to the window as Blüstav floated away. Lettie felt like he had hooks in her heart, because watching him she felt a wrenching, tearing, rending inside, worse than anything she had ever felt before. He was pulling out her hope, Lettie realized; the hope she had always carried, its roots went so deep. But now Ma and the snow cloud were lost, and Lettie was marooned on the top of an iceberg.

"What's left?" she said to Noah through her tears. "What's left to hope for now?"

Noah couldn't answer.

Ma couldn't guide her.

With no one else to turn to, Lettie looked at the horizon for someone to come.

Please, God, she prayed. *Send someone. Anyone.*

Then she spotted them.

"Anyone but them!" she cried out. "Anyone but them!"

She grabbed her telescope, pulled it open, and watched the *Bloodbucket* as it hurtled toward the iceberg, spitting fire and smoke.

How had the crones tracked them through the clouds, all the way to the iceberg? It was the Goggler's scopical glasses. It had to be. Lettie watched her from the deck. Her hair was soggy (from where the Walrus had dunked her), and the whalers had fixed her glasses together with string and spit. She was standing well away from the Walrus, whose piggy eyes glared.

Then the Goggler began to jump and point straight at Blüstav. And Blubber Johnson cranked the harpoon gun up toward the alchemist.

"Oh, no!" said Lettie.

"If that harpoon hits Blüstav, he'll be skewered," said Noah, and Lettie winced. No matter what Blüstav had just done, she couldn't wish something that gruesome on *anybody*.

"I can't watch!" she said, shutting her eyes as Blubber Johnson fired.

"Missed!" cried Noah instantly, and Lettie looked up to see the harpoon already far past Blüstav and arcing back down into the sea. The alchemist swam through the air as fast as he could, rising up and up, toward the safety of a cloud. He kicked his legs and flailed his arms, but his limbs were still strung with Noah's vines, so his strokes were rather feeble.

"He'll escape," said Lettie, looking back to the *Bloodbucket*. "They're used to fishing things from the sea, not the sky."

As Blubber Johnson loaded another harpoon the Goggler elbowed him away, taking the gun and aiming it herself.

"*She* won't miss," said Noah. "Not with those scopical glasses."

Steam spurted from the gun, and the harpoon shot into the air. It flew up, a gigantic arrow of iron, coursed to pluck Blüstav from the sky. The higher it got, the slower it went as gravity pulled it back down. It stopped, barely five feet below the alchemist's wriggling feet, before it began to fall.

"She missed!" said Noah, utterly mystified. "I don't believe it!"

But, Lettie realized a moment later, the Goggler had not been aiming for Blüstav at all. She had aimed for a far larger target: *the canopy of vines below him.*

The harpoon dropped into the very same tangle of vines that the suitcase had hung in an hour beforehand. It stretched them taut as harp strings, but not one of them snapped. Noah had grown them far too strong.

"Very clever," said Noah, a touch of admiration in his voice. "If she had aimed for Blüstav, the harpoon would have pierced his coat and the cloud would have escaped."

"Yes," said Lettie bitterly. "This way, the crones get snow *and* their revenge."

The harpoon lay in the canopy. Blüstav still swam

and kicked and flailed, until the veins on his neck stood out like cords. But he could do nothing to stop himself from sinking slowly down to the *Bloodbucket*, where two old ladies prowled upon the deck like wild animals. Restless. Hungry.

Keeping her telescope on Blüstav, Lettie couldn't help feeling that he would devise some new, miraculous means of escape. Sure enough, she watched him edge his fingers round the curve of his coat toward a pocket. He stretched and strained, all the while sinking closer to the deck of the *Bloodbucket*, where Grot-Nose Charlie waited with a net and Captain McNulty popped the lid off an empty barrel.

"That must be what they're planning to put the snow cloud in," said Noah. "After they pry it out of Blüstav."

Lettie grimaced. She closed her eyes and tried to feel Ma. Nothing. There was nothing she could do but stand at the window and watch. It made her think back to her old life, at the White Horse Inn. How horrible and frustrating it was!

She willed Blüstav's fingers into that pocket. The alchemist was barely ten feet from the deck.

"Come on . . . Almost there . . ."

Suddenly his fingers were in, and closing around something: a bottle! He had one alchemical left, but what was it? Lettie thought she had used them all aboard *Leutha's Wood*. But, no . . . She recognized this one: Blüstav had used it before, on the Walrus and on Da. It was gastromajus, the alchemical that turned a person into their last meal.

At once the crones leaped back, terrified. The Walrus covered her head and the Goggler dived under Captain McNulty's legs. But Blüstav unscrewed the bottle and held it to his own mouth.

"He's using it on himself!" Noah cried.

And ten feet above the deck, Blüstav let three pink drops fall upon his tongue and tipped the rest over his head. It poured down his coat, soaking him from head to foot.

Black smoke billowed. Green sparks flew. His head shrank and his body grew. His coat turned gray and began to blister.

"What is he becoming?" Lettie wondered aloud.

Noah frowned. "He didn't have any tea just now."

"I don't think I've ever seen him eat *anything*," said Lettie.

"I'm sure *I* have. But what was it?"

And Noah and Lettie cast back into their minds

to catch the memory, like a pair of fishermen throwing their lines downstream, until at once they both shouted aloud:

"Clams on *Leutha's Wood*!"

Looking back, Lettie saw the smoke clear. Blüstav had vanished, and in his place was a speckled black oval, three feet wide. Through the eye of the telescope, the clam looked like the egg of some colossal chicken. Blüstav tumbled down onto the deck, landing with a crunch on the wooden planks.

Blüstav the liar, thought Lettie. *Blüstav the thief, Blüstav the cheat . . . and now, Blüstav the clam.*

"He's trapped the snow cloud inside his shell," said Noah. "He's *swallowed* it."

On the deck of the *Bloodbucket*, the Goggler peered out from beneath Captain McNulty. The Walrus crept as close as she could to the clam. Grot-Nose Charlie sharpened his dagger on his boot and grinned.

"They're going to pry it out of him, though," said Lettie, shaking her head. "I can't stand this watching, Noah! We have to *do* something!"

"Do what, Lettie?" The leaves on his shoulder were curling with frustration. She could see his green eyes searching her for something: a plan, an idea, *anything*.

"I don't know, Noah!" She almost howled it. "Blüstav

is there, and we're here, and Ma has vanished, and we can't change a thing."

"We *must* be able to," said Noah. "It's the first rule of alchemy: *things change*."

And then she saw it: a spark of something in his eyes.

And then she *felt* the spark too, in her heart. A flicker of something . . . an ember of hope.

"I think . . . " she bit her lip, " . . . I think I have an idea. It might be impossible—"

Noah laughed. "Lettie, I don't believe in 'impossible,' and neither do you!" He gripped her arm. "Tell me how we get the snow back."

"It's simple really," Lettie found herself saying. "We're going to go over to the *Bloodbucket*, and fight for it!"

"It's an awfully long way to swim," said Noah.

"Then we're going to need awfully big flippers," said Lettie as she took his hand. "Come on!"

Lettie Peppercorn
Stitches the Waves

Lettie pulled Noah over to the cauldron, and together
they emptied out the dregs of tea.

"We're going to do some alchemy," she told him.
"Something that will make us strong enough to swim
over there and *fight*!"

"Yes!" he cried. His eyes flickered across the floor
at all of the strewn-about papers. "Where's the recipe
we're using?"

"No time for recipes, Noah. We'll just do what feels
right."

"But we need books for alchemy," insisted Noah.
"And alchemicals, and your ma to help us, and—"

"All we need is imagination," insisted Lettie. "How hard can it be? First, choose the ingredients. Second, mix them together. Finally, decide how much to drink."

Noah laughed. "When you put it like that, it sounds easy!"

Lettie laughed too and a jitter of adrenaline ran through her. This might work! "Get the fire roaring, and I'll find us some things to mix."

"Wait a minute, Lettie. What are we turning ourselves into?"

Lettie shrugged. "Something strong enough to swim through that freezing sea; something big enough to take on the *Bloodbucket*. But I can't tell you *exactly* what it will be yet . . . wait and see. Do you trust me?"

"Of course I do!" said Noah. "I saw you on *Leutha's Wood* with all those alchemicals."

Lettie felt herself turning red. "I was just following Ma."

"You still managed something incredible," said Noah. "You've got your ma's talent. You're made from alchemy yourself. You'll do this. I know you will."

Lettie felt a huge swell of pride. Noah trusted her, and that was enough. She turned away from him and began to scour the room for ingredients.

"Choose anything," she breathed to herself. "As long as it feels *right*."

She started with water: scraping flakes of ice from the window and leaving them to melt in the cauldron. After that she flicked through some books lying scattered on the floor, but they were all useless and very boring. She stripped the leather covers from twenty of them—she liked how tough they were—and left them all in a pile. Sifting around in one of the other rooms, she found a tiny glass bell unbroken. It looked so lonely there among its shattered friends that she couldn't resist picking it up.

Back in the laboratory, she found a whole trove of lost things: a green marble and some rubber bands down one of the armchairs, and a silk paintbrush, a silver shilling, and a compass. She took the needle from the compass and the silk threads from the paintbrush, but she left everything else because it was junk. If she added too many useless things, the alchemy wouldn't work.

That was everything from the floor. She turned her attention to the ceiling.

Something caught her eye at once. She found an old stepladder, climbed it, and took a glittering shard from the icicle chandelier above. It was beautiful, and hard as a diamond. She slipped it in her pocket and jumped to the floor.

There was something else: a missing ingredient. She wondered what it was. It had something to do with the glass bell.

"Music!" she cried suddenly. "I'll get that in a moment."

Lettie knew somehow that all the ingredients had been gathered, and it was time now to mix them. She went back to the cauldron, where the water simmered and Noah made the bellows wheeze.

"I've done the choosing," Lettie told him. "Now for the mixing."

With her compass needle, Lettie began to weave through the water from North to East to South to West. She wanted to stitch the ripples together into spirals. She sewed and sewed, until her fingers ached and she had to stop.

"The water's stirring itself," said Noah, full of awe. "How is it doing that?"

"I've stitched it into spirals, see?" Lettie explained. "North to East to South to West."

The cauldron now held a miniature whirlpool. It was time for Lettie's next ingredient. She took the needle and pricked a tiny hole in the glass bell.

"Sing into this, Noah," she said. "A song you know. A song that feels right."

While he thought about what to sing, Lettie took the silk threads from her pocket and poked them inside the bell. They would soak up the song and keep it there, Lettie was sure of it.

"Are you ready?" she said to him, holding out the bell.

Shyly, Noah began to sing. It was the hundredth verse of a song that Lettie knew; she had heard it days before, standing outside the Clam Before the Storm:

> *"The albatross, her wings unfurled*
> *Called to him, as off she flew:*
> *'The sea will wash away the world,*
> *The world will rise again, anew.*
> *But oh, to your own self be true!*
> *To your own self be true!'"*

Noah finished, his voice sweet and nervous, and then he covered the hole with his thumb.

When Lettie told him he held it over the cauldron and let it fall into the whirlpool.

"That'll spread your song through the water," said Lettie, as the bell whirled all the way down to the bottom.

"It will?" said Noah, quite bewildered.

"Of course! Now keep that fire going!" she ordered.

So Noah worked the bellows while Lettie dangled the tough leather book covers into the cauldron, one by one, until they went limp and lifeless—then she threw them away.

"How much longer?" Noah puffed.

"Nearly done. Although there's something else to add, but I can't think what it is . . ."

Lettie ran her fingers through her pockets and—*ouch!*—pricked herself on the chandelier shard. With a hiss, she stuck her thumb in her mouth, withdrawing it slowly to look at the damage. A bright bead of blood trembled on the end, and before she could stop it, it fell down into the cauldron, staining the water ruby red. The water whirled faster and faster, until it was just a blur.

"Oh, no!" said Noah. "Do we start again?"

"Actually, I think I need a drop from *you* too."

"Why?"

"Think about it, Noah. *We* have to be in this alchemy as well. Otherwise it might work *too* well. We'll stop being Lettie and Noah . . . we might forget we ever *were* children."

"We wouldn't care about getting snow back."

"We might not even *remember* our plan," said Lettie. "We might just want to swim around all day."

Taking the shard, she drew a bead of blood from Noah's thumb and shook it into the cauldron. The whirlpool swallowed it greedily.

And then stopped.

The two of them stood, looking at their alchemy. It had turned the color of milk and the consistency of honey.

"It's ready, isn't it?" said Noah. He was hopping from foot to foot in excitement.

"Not yet. There's one last thing to add." Lettie reached for the salt pot from the table, turned it upside down, and shook it all over the cauldron.

"Even alchemy needs seasoning," she said.

Noah sucked his thumb and laughed. "This is just like making soup."

"You're right," said Lettie. "But who's going to test it?"

"Me first," said Noah.

"Shouldn't we toss a coin?" said Lettie, reaching for the shilling by the armchair.

"Don't be silly. *You're* the alchemist, Lettie. I just worked the bellows. If something goes wrong I'll need *you* to change me back."

Lettie gulped. Perhaps she should have searched the

shelf for a recipe. But it was too late now. She had trusted herself to pick the ingredients and mix them together . . . now she needed to trust Noah. She knew he was right.

"All right," she said at last. "You first."

"What should I do?" said Noah. "Drink it?"

"No," said Lettie. "It probably tastes disgusting."

"I could get inside the cauldron?" Noah suggested. "Like it's a bathtub?"

Lettie shrugged. "I was in charge of choosing and mixing," she said. "You're in charge of testing. You decide."

"All right," said Noah. "I'll swim in it." He put out the fire and waited for the cauldron to cool. Then he sat on an armchair and took off his shoes and socks.

"What are you doing?"

"I'm leaving my clothes here, so when you change me back I can just step into them again."

"Oh," said Lettie. "That's a sensible idea."

Noah nodded, put his socks in his shoes, and then sat for a long moment, waiting.

Waiting for what?

"Do you mind?" he asked.

"Do I mind what?" Lettie felt herself turning red, though she couldn't understand why.

Now Noah was turning red too. This was all most peculiar. "Do you mind looking over there, or something?" he said.

"Oh!" said Lettie. "Oh!"

They both said at the same time: "Sorry!"

Then: "Don't be sorry!"

Then: "No, *I'm* the one who—"

Then they both burst out laughing.

For the next few minutes, Lettie stared very, very intently at the door handle.

"Don't look!" came Noah's voice.

"*Eurgh!* I'm not looking," said Lettie. "I'm having second thoughts."

"About what?"

"About the alchemy, of course!" she snapped. "I didn't follow a recipe, Noah. I didn't follow anything at all!"

"You followed your imagination."

"Yes!" said Lettie, panicked. "What a stupid thing to do! I should have followed *instructions*! I should have followed *Ma*! I'm not an alchemist, I'm twelve!"

"You're Lettie Peppercorn," said Noah simply. "Alchemy is a part of you. It's in your blood. And that's good enough for me."

And before she could say another word, his feet

pattered across the floor and he splashed into the cauldron.

"Noah?" she cried, whirling round. "Did it work?"

It took Lettie only a second to pivot on her heel and shout, but in that tiny moment it had already begun.

There was a blinding *FLASH*, a deafening *SCREECH*, and the cauldron tore in two. The alchemy whirled up in a spout, and Noah inside it grew, and grew, and grew.

Lettie let out an exhilarating shout. The alchemy had worked spectacularly. *Her* alchemy! She had picked, mixed, and made a potion, and now Noah was changing in front of her eyes. . . .

Changing into what, though?

Something big. Big enough to squash her flat if she didn't move quick.

Lettie Peppercorn, RUN!

A Mighty BOOM
Interrupts Dinner

On the *Bloodbucket*, the Goggler and the Walrus were dining on the deck. Captain McNulty lifted a crate from below and laid a rancid tablecloth over it. The crones sat scowling as Grot-Nose Charlie tried for the hundred and fifteenth time to pry open Blüstav's mouth with a hammer and chisel.

"How much longer will this take?" spat the Goggler.

"Grot-Nose Charlie will have that cloud out but momentarily," said Captain McNulty. "Else I'll be giving him a piece of my wrath and the point of my harpoon. In the meantime, dinner is served!"

"I've had enough of sea biscuits," muttered the Walrus.

"Then feast yer eyes and yer appetites on *this*," the captain said to the crones, giving them his biggest, bloodiest smile. He called Blubber Johnson from the kitchen, who arrived carrying a large tin platter, lidded and steaming.

The captain lifted the lid and there, on a bed of seaweed, lay a lobster.

"Lovely and fresh!" he exclaimed. "Still twitchin', just the way it should be."

The Goggler looked at the lobster, her eyes as big as plates. The Walrus smacked her lips. They had been upon the sea for days, with nothing to eat but stale water and biscuits. But *here* was a meal fit for royalty. They seized their forks and began to guzzle the poor thing, shell and all.

"They've the manners of a pair of seagulls," murmured Blubber Johnson to his captain.

"Aye. But it keeps them off our backs for a few moments longer."

"Do you think they'd be guzzling it so, if they knew where we got it from?"

Captain McNulty grinned. The lobster had been cut from the belly of the last whale they had caught. "Let's not tell them that, shall we? Grot-Nose!" he shouted. "Are ye any closer to cracking that there clam?"

For the hundred and seventeenth time, the whaler smote the hammer upon the chisel, but Blüstav's jaws stayed firmly shut. Grot-Nose Charlie dropped the chisel and sat, wiping his weeping nostrils. "I got no more hammering in me," he wheezed.

"Yer a tough one," said the captain, kneeling beside Blüstav. "I give ye that. But if you don't open those jaws of yours, I'll fetch me my bazooka. I ain't never seen a crack that can't be conjured with dynamite."

He waited on the clam, but the clam stayed shut.

"That's it decided, then," growled the captain, standing and striding toward his bazooka. "I'll swear it right now, there's about to be a *mighty BOOM* around here!"

Captain McNulty was right, in a way. There did come a *mighty BOOM* that rolled over the ship like a wave and shook the crones from their guzzling.

"What was that?" said the Walrus, bits of shell quivering on her chin.

Above the *Bloodbucket*, part of the iceberg had exploded in a firework of colors, and a small boy was tumbling from an iceberg window, along with the two halves of an iron cauldron.

The crones and crew of the *Bloodbucket* watched him falling. He slid and tumbled down the ice peaks and the broken spires.

"That's him!" said Blubber Johnson. "The small lad with the twig."

"Rot," said Grot-Nose Charlie. "He's a big-'un."

"He looks bigger than 'e did a second ago," said Blubber Johnson.

"That's cos he's closer," said Captain McNulty. "They call that prospective."

"Don't ye mean *perspective*, Captain?" asked Blubber Johnson.

"Shut yer trap!" bellowed Captain McNulty, and he coughed up a glob of red spit right in Blubber Johnson's eye.

"He looks massive now," said Grot-Nose Charlie.

"Aye," said the captain. He licked the blood off his gums and grinned. "That's prospective for ye."

"Thirty feet tall."

"An' he's got himself a flipper."

"What are you talking about, idiots?" said Captain McNulty. He held up his telescope for a closer look, but all he saw was a splash as Noah hit the sea.

"That was a big splash for one small boy."

"He weren't a boy when he hit those waves," said Grot-Nose Charlie nervously.

"What was he then?" said Blubber Johnson.

They might have stood and pondered the question

a good while longer, but the whalers' attention was drawn to the iceberg as the tip of it toppled and slid smoothly into the sea.

"Take us back!" called Captain McNulty to Stoker Pete, and the propellers began to hum in reverse. The *Bloodbucket* reversed away from the falling, crashing, splashing ice.

"That boy is drowned for sure," said Blubber Johnson.

"And what of the girl?" Captain McNulty asked. "No one saw her."

Grot-Nose Charlie shrugged. "If she isn't crushed by the ice, she'll be swallowed by the sea."

"You are sure?" said the Goggler.

"Sure as I can be. The sea is a thirsty thing. It gulps down whatever it can."

The Goggler grinned and wiped the lobster flesh from her lips. "How excellent! That is the last of the witnesses. We are done here. Take your time prying open that clam, gentlemen. Captain McNulty, set us on a course back to Barter!"

Noah Will Come

The laboratory slid down the iceberg in one big chunk and struck the surface of the sea like a hand slapping a drum. Water poured in. All Lettie could hear was ringing and all she could see was darkness and bubbles, and she could taste nothing but salt. And which way was up? Which way was up? Oh it was cold, so cold, like swimming in æther.

Lettie Peppercorn, don't you drown. Swim up and find something to hold on to. Noah will come. Noah will come.

Her fingers found the rim of the open window and she swam through. The currents were swirling and tossing her up to the surface, then back down. Playing with her.

Then she broke the surface, gulping air and kicking with all her might to stay afloat and alive. Wiping the hair from her eyes, she looked for something to cling onto while she waited for Noah—or whatever Noah had become. But there was nothing but foam and rolling waves, and all the while her legs were growing weaker and Da in her coat pocket was heavy, and each breath was harder to take.

Lettie sank underwater again, the sea churning in her ears and eyes and mouth. She flailed her fists but the cold had taken all her strength. Bit by bit the surface grew farther and farther away. Her legs were numb and gone and she no longer knew if they were still kicking or whether they had given in.

That was when Noah found her, lifting her up with a great blue fin to the surface of the water, where she lay still and cold until, at last, she coughed and spluttered and breathed.

Lettie floated, catching her breath for a long time. Glass bells and bits of armchair bobbed past among the floes of ice. Lettie looked at the fin and then she gazed up, startled, into an eye that was bigger than she was; verdant green and somehow shy, despite its size.

"Noah?" she said. "Is that you?"

But she already knew it was, for sprouting from the

top of his gigantic body was his stalk, only now it had become a fully grown tree.

"Just look at you!" she said, hugging the trunk. "You're a whale! And your shoot's become a tree! Now we can *do* something!"

Noah crooned low and swam forward. They rounded the iceberg in a moment, and Lettie saw the *Bloodbucket* in the distance, sailing away.

"They think they've won!" she said furiously. "They think they've beaten us. Well, we'll show them! Let's get them, Noah! Let's smash that rusty ship to bits!"

He surged toward the *Bloodbucket*.

"What can I do, Noah?" said Lettie as he swam. "You can swipe your tail and butt your head, but I'm still twelve."

In reply, Noah rustled his branches. Growing among the leaves were coconuts and prickly pears. Lettie clambered up the trunk and into his canopy. The *Bloodbucket* was only a few hundred yards away. Lettie steadied the jitters running through her. She had to be the quickest, fiercest, and luckiest she had ever been. The crones would shoot their terrible guns and the whalers would throw their harpoons. There was no Ma to take her hand and rescue her.

Noah sank deeper in the water as he closed in on the whalers, until the only thing left above the waves was his tree—with Lettie in the branches.

Her hands shook as she picked coconuts into a pile in her lap. And ahead the *Bloodbucket* drew closer. Closer.

Lettie Peppercorn, don't you tremble.

The Walrus was on deck, savoring her last scraps of lobster, when the wind brought her something impossible.

It blew a flat, green leaf onto her plate.

She trapped it with her fork before it could be carried off again. She stared at it with her black, piggy eyes. Finding a leaf out here in the middle of the ocean, thought the Walrus, was like finding a sunset in the middle of the night, or mustard in the middle of a Victoria sponge cake. It just *didn't belong*.

Where had the leaf come from?

"Look at this," she said to the Goggler.

The Goggler stared, long and hard. "A leaf? Miles from land? We must be hallucinating. That can happen when you eat too much lobster."

"Perhaps," said the Walrus, knowing this was not the case because she was still hungry.

"How did it get there?" said the Goggler, glaring at the leaf.

"The wind brought it," said the Walrus. "From behind us—"

They turned around just in time to see the coconut.

Justice Is Served

The coconut flew through the air and hit Grot-Nose Charlie right on his grotty nose. He fell on the deck sobbing and swearing, while the little girl who had thrown it laughed and cheered on her tree branch.

The crones gawped. It was their landlady, sitting in the branches of a leafy green tree whose roots vanished into the water. And, even more unfathomable, this tree was *moving* alongside the ship.

"We've got cabin fever!" cried Blubber Johnson.

"We're going mad!" yelled Captain McNulty in terror.

"We were *mad* days ago," said the Walrus. "Now, we are *furious.*"

"You should have drowned when you had the chance," snarled the Goggler, whipping out her silver pistol and sidestepping a coconut.

Lettie didn't answer. Noah did. He reared from his hiding place below the sea and butted the *Bloodbucket* with all his strength. The ship screamed and buckled and tossed everyone onboard in the air like salad leaves.

While they were dazed, Noah swam up beside the ship and Lettie jumped aboard from her branch. The crones lay beside her, groaning. The Walrus had spilled tea from her head all down her dress and the Goggler was squinting and searching for her scopical glasses that lay on the floor by her feet.

Lettie ignored them. Only Blüstav mattered. There he was, on the far side of the deck! She ran but tripped on something: the Goggler had her boot in a bony grip.

"Just look what I've caught!" She cackled.

Lettie squirmed but couldn't get free. She shouldn't have tied her laces so tight! The Goggler pulled her closer and closer, until Lettie could smell the perfume on the old woman's neck and the lobster on her breath. She threw Lettie to the floor.

"I won't need my glasses from this distance," she hissed, the silver pistol in her hand.

Noah was wrestling with the *Bloodbucket*'s crane: Blubber Johnson had made it to the controls and wrapped the iron claw around Noah's tail. Noah strained and twisted but the crane held—it was bolted to the deck. Now it had Noah trapped, and slowly Blubber Johnson began to hoist him from the water!

In desperation, Noah the whale threw his whole weight at the ship again. It was then that the Goggler aimed her pistol. The *Bloodbucket* rocked, and the old crone teetered off balance. Lettie saw her chance, and kicked. The Goggler staggered back, trod on a rolling coconut, and sat down in a heap. Lettie heard the *CRUNCH* of glass as she hit the deck. The Goggler screamed a steady stream of Bohemian curses that dissolved into a steady stream of salty tears. Underneath her, the scopical glasses had splintered into one hundred pieces, and each piece was horribly jagged and ever so pointy.

Lettie left her weeping and wailing and carried on searching for Blüstav. She knew she had to be quick. The whalers were busy fighting Noah, and by the looks of things they were winning. Though Noah was rocking the *Bloodbucket* back and forth, he was trapped by the crane. Just one shot from the bazooka would blow him to smithereens.

On the far side of the boat, Captain McNulty seemed to have exactly the same thought. He locked eyes with Lettie. Then both of them looked at the bazooka lying between them. Lettie staggered toward it as the deck seesawed under her feet. The crane cogs screamed and Noah roared and the bazooka lay silent, waiting to see who would claim it.

Lettie started off closest, but Captain McNulty had sea legs; the rocking of the boat had no effect on him. Her insides dropped as he strolled up to the bazooka and bent down to scoop it up.

But then there was a *BANG*, and his eyes bulged in agony. The Goggler, half-blind with pain, rage, and short-sightedness, had seen two blurs in front of her and fired her pistol.

Unfortunately for Captain McNulty, she had picked the wrong blur. The bullet whizzed straight through his boot. He howled and spat and swore and made one last grab for the bazooka, but Lettie whipped it away from his grasp. Hefting it in her hands, she aimed without thinking and squeezed the trigger.

The tiny dynamite stick flew from the barrel of the bazooka, landing at the foot of the crane. Blubber Johnson didn't even notice it there as the fuse hissed away to nothing and the stick went . . .

BOOM!

The explosion threw up sparks and smoke, lifting the crane into the air as if it were a firework. Suddenly it was no longer attached to the *Bloodbucket* and Noah was no longer trapped. He saw his chance. Jerking his tail back, he flattened the crane with a heavy swat, stabbing it down through the *Bloodbucket*'s deck.

Never before in seafaring history had a whale harpooned a whaling ship. The crane pierced the hull, the sea came up like a fountain, and the whalers (those who were left) cried out, "Abandon ship!"

Grot-Nose Charlie ran for the lifeboat, holding his nose. Captain McNulty hopped after him. Stoker Pete came up from the engine rooms and dove into the waves headfirst, almost as if he was relieved to be finally having a wash. But Lettie did not watch them: she scoured the deck for Blüstav the clam.

The sea splattered and sprayed as it gobbled up the ship, spitting foam like saliva over Lettie's feet. She began to panic. He wasn't anywhere! There were floating barrels, harpoons, lifejackets, and Blubber Johnson's boots . . . but no Blüstav. She only had a few minutes, and she couldn't see him. Lettie froze in fear. What if he sank into the sea along with the ship? The cloud would be gone forever.

She caught a glimpse of something black, lodged between two crates at the sinking end of the ship. It was him! Dragging Blüstav free, she rolled him to where the deck was still dry. Her hands were shaking. His shell was as black as his coat had been, and Lettie ran her hands over it, feeling rough bumps and raised patches that had once been buttons and pockets. She had Blüstav, now she had to find a way to make him open and give back the snow he had stolen for so long. The crones hadn't made him. Not even Ma had made him. How could Lettie?

She searched the littered deck for things to use. She tried prying him open with a rope and a pulley, but he stayed shut. And the water rose higher.

Lettie pressed her ear to his shell. She heard rumblings inside of him. She heard his fear and his greed. She began to whisper, but not to Blüstav. She spoke to the cloud.

"Hello, cloud. You're angry, aren't you? I can hear your rumbling. I've seen your thunder. You're trapped. I know how that feels, cloud. I've been trapped just as long as you, you see."

Underneath Blüstav's shell, the cloud stopped its thunder. As if it was listening. Lettie surged on: "But we can help each other, cloud. We can set each other free. When you're free in the sky, I'll be free on the ground. I'll never trap you, I'll let you spread out across the world and make snow wherever you want. But you have to help me now. I can't get you out all on my own."

And Lettie heard the cloud start to rumble, and felt Blüstav start to shake, harder and harder.

"That's it!" she shouted. "Struggle, cloud! Wriggle your way out! Work your way free! I know you can do it!"

And the cloud fought, fought to be free . . . And Lettie fought too, with every ounce of her strength, to force Blüstav open . . . And the cloud thundered and roared . . . And Lettie pulled and sweated and pulled, and finally, she felt Blüstav give in.

He opened an inch, and her hands trembled as he struggled to shut again. There was the snow cloud, squashed tightly behind his jaws like a pearl.

But now that Blüstav was open, it could escape: the cloud billowed away at last and rose into the air.

It looked different. It had spent so long swallowed up in Blüstav's coat that it had turned pink.

Why pink? Lettie wondered.

And she realized just in time. Pink was the color of the gastromajus that Blüstav had swallowed! The cloud had soaked it up like a sponge, and now it was free, it was ready to spit it all out again.

Lettie Peppercorn, you get to shelter!

She dove to the ground as the cloud swept over her, dark and spitting, brewing up a blizzard. But this snowstorm would change anyone it touched; change them into their last meal!

Lettie ran for cover. The cloud rose above the deck. She had to get away before it snowed. She ran past the crones as the ship pitched and sank. There! Noah swam to her left, circling the *Bloodbucket* anxiously. She cried out to him and he sidled up, so she could jump on. A fat, pink snowflake drifted just by her foot as she leaped for his tree.

"The girl!" cried the Walrus.

"Never mind the girl," said the Goggler. "Look at the cloud! It's out! It's out and right above our heads!"

The cloud thundered and swelled, full to bursting.

"Snow for us, cloud!" the Goggler cried. With her scopical glasses on, she would have spotted that the cloud was full of gastromajus in an instant. But she was blind, and the Walrus was stupid, so they raised their hands up to the peals of thunder and danced with jubilation.

"Snow!" they began to chant. "Snow! Snow! Snow!"

They were still chanting when the cloud split, covering them head to toe in a thick blanket of pink alchemicals.

Noah's leaves shielded Lettie from harm, and she huddled around the trunk and watched the gastromajus tumble down onto the Goggler and the Walrus. Howling, screaming, they ran for cover but it was no use. They were in the midst of the blizzard, and the alchemy was working.

Lettie saw their faces turn gray and their hands become claws. She saw their eyes become black balls on stalks, their skin turn to shell. It was horrible to watch, but no more than they deserved. The old crones had become a pair of big, gray lobsters; they scuttled into the waves, sank to the bottom of the ocean, and were never seen by Lettie again. (They spent the rest of their days skulking among the muck of the sea floor, consumed by jealousy and meanness, evicting hermit crabs from their shells, until they were both caught in a fisherman's trap and served at the wedding feast of Her Royal Highness Princess Josefin of Laplönd. Very bitter, tasteless, and gristly lobsters they were too, and many of the guests complained to Princess Josefin, who cried and stamped her feet and nearly executed the chef. But she spared his life and forgave him everything, for when he scrutinized the lobsters to see what was wrong he found five gold rings on the claw of one, and a chandelier earring hanging from the other.)

Lettie watched the *Bloodbucket* slipping away. With a last gurgle it was gone. The whalers, far off in the rowing boat, began the long journey back to land.

"Serves them right for what they did to your grandma," said Lettie to Noah. "For what they tried to do to us."

She felt no pity in her heart for those cruel and vicious men. They had learned a valuable lesson: never pick on whales, or small children—one day they'll decide to fight back, and then you'll be sorry.

"Let's go home," she said, reaching into her apron to touch Da. Noah turned and swam south toward land. Toward Albion and Barter.

And following them drifted the snow cloud. It had snowed away every last drop of gastromajus. It had thundered away its anger at being trapped for ten years. Now it was a color Lettie had never seen it before. Now it was white.

The Awful Loneliness Returns

Noah swam for two days, with Lettie in his branches. He grew apples for her to eat, and when she became sick of apples, he grew pears. Lettie spent the daytime climbing and talking to Noah. She told him her whole life: about Periwinkle and Da and her home on stilts. At night she watched the stars if they were out. But sometimes the snow cloud was in the way, and then she had nothing but her thoughts of Ma.

Sometimes Lettie thought of Blüstav too, somewhere at the bottom of the sea, tossed by underwater currents. She couldn't help feeling sorry for him, despite what he had done. He didn't deserve to be a clam, down in the deeps, all alone.

She first knew they were nearing Barter when she saw Albion's gray cliffs against the horizon. As Noah swam up, she could see the familiar shape of the valley and the first faint spires of the ships. Lettie sat watching the miniature town grow and grow, until at last Noah surged into the harbor. There were the cobbled roads and slate houses. Everything smudged a dirty gray or dull green. There were some traders selling fish on the quay. There was the smell of vinegar. There was the *clippety-clop* of hooves. A few children on the beach were staring. Many ships had come into the harbor, but never a whale.

Noah swam right up to the harborside, and stopped. He lowered his tree until Lettie could step lightly onto the shore. But she didn't. She clung to him.

He waited. He shook his branches gently, but Lettie wouldn't budge. In her heart was a feeling she hadn't felt since leaving Barter: her loneliness had come back.

Because, after everything, Ma was still somewhere *out there*.

And Da was still a beer bottle.

And Noah was still a whale.

It was Noah who terrified her the most, because

deep in her heart she knew what had to happen. He had to swim away, swim away and leave her. She could feel it in the silence between them like distance.

With Noah she had unlocked the secret of snow; the secrets of alchemy. With him, Lettie had shared everything: battles, escapes, starry nights, stories, and chili soup. If he left, she would have nothing. Her only friend would be the cloud above her head.

It was all the fault of stupid alchemy.

"Stupid stupid stupid," she muttered. And then she shouted, so loud the fishermen jumped and ran from their stalls: "WHY CAN'T THINGS STAY THE SAME? My life was boring and sad but I'd gotten used to it. But then I got all hopeful that things were going to change for the better, and they *haven't*, and now I think everything is just worse and I can't take finding a family and a friend and then losing them all again."

She sat in the tree and cried for a bit, feeling miserable and lonely.

"Oh, Noah," she wept. "I want the old you. I want you back the way you were. I don't want a whale for a friend. I don't want a beer bottle for a da. I don't want a ma made of air. I don't want to be a stone. And you can't say anything to make me feel better."

Noah shifted uneasily in the water, and then he dove.

"And I don't want to drown, either," she said loudly, but he ignored her. She held on to the branches and took a deep breath.

As soon as her ears were under the water she heard him. He was singing, but it was unlike anything she had ever heard before. Noah's whale song was strange and powerful and sad and beautiful. It made all the water buzz and shake around her. Listening to it, she felt she understood: Noah was sad to be leaving her, but he was saying *thank you*. He loved being a whale.

Then his singing stopped and they came back up. She gasped for breath as the water ran cold and freezing from the tree and the sun began slowly to dry her.

"Thank you too, Noah," she said, wringing the water from her coat. She stepped from his branches. "I don't know how you did it, but you've made me feel better, somehow."

Noah shrugged his fins, as if to say: *That's what friends are for.*

"I wonder how long my alchemy will last," she said to him. "How long will I have to wait for you to become a boy again?"

Noah shrugged his fins again, as if to say: *No alchemy lasts forever.*

Realizing that made her feel even better. "You've cheered me up without saying a word!" she laughed. "Just how do you do it?"

He didn't have to say it or sing it. Lettie just knew.

She asked two hundred and twelve times why he was leaving.

"And I'll keep asking until I get an answer I'm satisfied with!" she said.

But, of course, he could never answer her, except in his strange underwater songs. By the water's edge, she tried to make him stay. She told him:

"You're my best friend."

And, "You saved my life."

And even, "You make better soup than me."

But Noah was going, and that was that. There are some things that just belong to the sea—whales are one of them, and Noah was another. Splashing his tail in farewell, he turned and left the harbor. He swam away, his tree leaves turning green to gold and red. They blew off on the breeze.

"I'll see you again, Noah!" she yelled. "Because no alchemy lasts forever! You won't always be a whale, but we'll always be friends, do you hear? I'll see you one day soon!"

Lettie stood there, shouting and crying and waving. She told him she'd never forget him. Never, ever, ever forget him. It was all she could say and she said it again and again and after that, she just waved.

She waved at Noah, then she waved at the ripples he left, then she waved at the waves. And when there was nothing left to wave at, she turned back to the town.

A Top Hat Wishes
to Be Borrowed

Lettie walked on through Barter as quickly as she could, all her thoughts on her petrifying feet. She even stepped on seaweed and fish heads rather than the cobbles. The wind was picking up, but it was no comfort anymore, just a cold nuisance. She held Da in her pocket, hidden away from any drunken sailors—she wasn't having any of them drink him. But the streets were almost empty.

"Well, well," said a voice from a doorway. "The landlady's back."

It was old Mr. Pity, the firewood seller. He was at the entrance of a tall, cozy-looking pub called the

Bargaining Bess with his ax by his ankles. A steaming cup of khave sat in his hands, a fluffy gray beard sat on his chin, and a top hat sat on his head.

"That's right," said Lettie. "I'm back."

"Wondered where you and your da had got to."

"I went to sea. Da came too."

"Hmm." Mr. Pity stroked his beard and tapped his foot. "Seeking treasure were you?"

"Sort of. I was looking for my ma."

"Ah," said Mr. Pity, holding his hat as the wind blew fierce. "Find her?"

"Yes," said Lettie. "But then she got lost again and my da is still a beer bottle, so I'm all on my own."

Mr. Pity looked concerned. "Don't you have any friends you could stay with?"

"My best friend lives in the sea."

Mr. Pity sipped his khave thoughtfully. "What about your second-best friend?"

"He's a pigeon."

"Ah, pity."

"He's at home right now, I bet. I should go see him, Mr. Pity. If I stay on these stones too long, I'll turn into one myself!"

"That's a troubling thought!" said Mr. Pity, leaning farther from the doorway of the Bargaining Bess.

"Well, my dear, if you ever get cold up in that house on stilts, you send me a message, and I'll be up with some kindling for you, free of charge."

Lettie waved and walked away. "Thank you! Goodbye! Stay warm!"

"You're welcome!" called Mr. Pity fondly. "*Adieu!* You too!"

And as Lettie left, he doffed his top hat. Suddenly the Wind howled, then *woompf!* It flew from his hands and landed in the gutter.

"Oh!" Mr. Pity cried as it slipped through his fingers.

"I'll get it," said Lettie, running to pick it up.

"*Psst.*"

Lettie stopped. What was that noise? The Wind?

"*Psst!*"

Whatever it was, it was coming from inside the hat.

"Lettie!"

Lettie's hand shot out and pinned the hat to the floor. Her heart was suddenly drumming in her chest. "Ma?"

"You got my top hat?" asked old Mr. Pity from the doorway. "Bring it here, miss."

Lettie picked it up, covering the end as carefully as she could, and turned to show it to him.

"Hello," said the hat.

Old Mr. Pity was about to sip his khave, but he jumped and tipped it into his beard instead.

"No need to jump," said the hat. "I just wanted to let you know, I'm being borrowed."

"Wha-what?" spluttered old Mr. Pity. "Why?"

"How do *I* know?" cried the hat. "I'm just a hat; I don't decide how long someone wears me for! Are you mad, or just stupid?"

Old Mr. Pity looked at the hat with wonder. "I had no idea you could talk," he said.

"Neither did I," said the hat. "But then this girl comes along, and all I know is I need to be borrowed! Never been one to shirk my duty, me, so off I go! I'm *needed.*"

"But you won't even fit her!" Mr. Pity protested. "Her head's tiny!"

"Well!" sniffed the hat. "That *is* rude! You don't hear *me* going on about the size of *your* head. Or your dandruff. Or the fact you've had the same haircut for fifty-seven years. Or the time you hid that ace of clubs underneath me so you could cheat at cards. Or the—"

Mr. Pity gave Lettie a look of utter helplessness. "Take it," he said. "Take it."

Lettie thanked him and began to walk away, but the

hat kept on. "I'll be back! Don't you think I won't be! But when I am, I want you to doff me to people in the street! And play cards fair! And hang me up on a hat stand with other hats! And get a haircut!"

Old Mr. Pity retreated inside the Bargaining Bess, and the hat started to laugh.

"Ma?" whispered Lettie. "Is that you?"

"Of course it is. Well, it's my head, anyway. What did you think of my acting skills back there?"

Lettie smiled for the first time since Noah had left. "I *knew* it was you! Poor Mr. Pity, he was lost for words!"

"Oh, he'll have his hat back soon. But I couldn't very well explain the *truth* to him, could I? Now carry me careful as you can. My legs are due any minute . . . can you see them?"

Lettie turned and laughed to see a pair of boots hopping up Vinegar Street toward her. She had her family back. It was the strangest family in Albion—maybe in all the world—but it was hers.

And once Lettie had taught Da how to wash up, and Ma how to make a good soup, things would be wonderful.

"Let's go home, Ma."

Lettie held her parents in her arms and laughed all

the way to the White Horse Inn. She was battered, bruised, and utterly exhausted, but somehow lighter. She wasn't lonely anymore.

The White Horse Inn was silent and empty: no rugs, no armchairs, no stove. Da had never showed at the Clam Before the Storm to pay his gambling debts, so Mr. Sleech the bailiff had come.

"It's horrible," said Lettie. "He even took the last rug."

"Just think of it as a blank slate," said Ma.

Then Lettie heard something: a faint *coo*.

"Periwinkle!" she cried. "Oh, Periwinkle, I'm back!"

She rushed into the kitchen, and there he was, sitting in his favorite spot, with his beak a little more cracked and his feathers a darker gray. Lettie smiled.

"Have I got a story to tell you, Peri!"

The Great Experiment Begins

In the weeks that followed there were lots more arrivals, and one departure worth telling of.

Ma's hands fell into a pair of feathered gloves on Tuesday. The rest of her tumbled in on an easterly breeze, and she was all back together by Friday. The first thing she did was take old Mr. Pity back his hat. Then she took Da in her hands and uncorked him. Lettie gasped.

"Don't worry, Lettie. I've not taken his head off," she said. "I just need to empty out all the gastromajus inside him."

Then she tipped all the beer and pink alchemical inside Da down the drain.

"Now we just have to wait," she said.

It happened a few hours later, by the hearth. Lettie came down the stairs to the sound of him snoring by the fire. He looked exactly the same as always—buttoned-up shirt, bow tie, and orange socks. And, just like Ma had promised, he did still have his head attached; only now among his red curls, Da had a bald patch.

"It's like the top of my hair just popped off," he said.

"It's exactly like that," laughed Lettie. Then she kissed him and called him Da and took his hand to show him Ma, who was waiting in boots and feathered gloves.

"First things first," said Ma. "You've been a bad father."

Da stared at his socks. "Can I ever make it up to you, Lettie?"

"Yes," said Lettie, hugging him.

Then she and Ma laughed, adding: "But do it *quickly!*"

The next arrival was a silent one. It happened at night. It came from the sky.

Snow came from the cloud, to dust the roofs of Barter white. People came out of their houses to stare at the snow. Children poked out their tongues to taste it.

When Lettie woke in the morning, Barter had changed. It had been wiped clean. Everywhere lay covered in snow. Billions and trillions of flakes had fallen, and were still falling.

"Look at that!" Lettie breathed onto her window. "It's white, pure white. It's like the ugly duckling turned into a swan."

She ran outside, cramming her arms into her coat as she went. The whole town was silent. Climbing down the ladder, she jumped the last rungs, and the snow made a crunch under her feet she would never forget. She smiled.

"And not a stone in sight," said Ma above her.

Lettie turned, laughing. Then she scooped up a handful of snow and threw it at Ma with all her might. There, on Vinegar Street, the world's first snowball fight began.

The last arrival happened on Barter beach, just after a storm. Da was picking through the flotsam for kindling when he found it. He heaved it onto the seafront and dragged it up Vinegar Street all by himself. It took him hours to roll it up the road, through the snow. As soon as he got to the well, he shouted for help.

Lettie's telescope had already spotted them from the kitchen window. "Da found him!" she yelled at a startled Periwinkle. "He found him, he found him, he found him!"

In minutes, Ma devised a pulley system from a few old ropes, three nails, and a tea towel, and they hoisted the clam inside. Lettie helped lift Blüstav up onto the table; Ma teased open his jaws with a feather and spoon, and all three of them emptied out the gastromajus that was still swilling around inside his shell.

"He'll change back soon," said Lettie. "We should leave a message for when he does."

"I know exactly what to write," said Ma.

And on a scrap of paper, she scribbled out:

A RECIPE FOR SNOW
A never-before-seen meteorological phenomenon

"You can't give him the recipe!" Lettie protested. "He'll just go back to tricking people!"

"I don't think so, Lettie," said Ma. "Snow is going to spread. We're going to take it to every place we can. You'll see. Soon, people will think it has fallen since the beginning of the world."

"Then why are you giving him the recipe?"

Ma put down the pen and folded the note beside Blüstav. "Because a recipe is only a guide, Lettie. If he can actually *make* snow, then he'll have no need for greed. He'll have found his imagination at last."

"Come on," said Da. "Pick up Periwinkle and let's go outside. There's something you need to see, Lettie."

They left Blüstav and crunched into the snow. It wasn't falling anymore. Lettie looked up. The sky was clearing and the cloud was moving east.

"We have to follow, don't we?" said Lettie.

Ma nodded. "Now the snow will start to melt. The stones around here won't be covered for long."

"But how will we survive?" said Lettie. "We've got no money, we've got no house, nothing."

"We'll go from village to town to city," said Da. "We'll follow the snow cloud. Who knows where we'll go?"

"Wherever the wind blows," Ma said.

"And where will that be?" said Da, getting excited. "Edenborg? Madri? Prais? Kiln?"

"It will be a great adventure!" said Ma. "The four of us are going to try and become a family."

"No!" said Lettie. "It *won't* be a great adventure, not one bit."

Her parents looked at their daughter with worried expressions.

"What will it be then?" said Da.

Lettie tightened her shoelaces, buttoned her coat, and perched Periwinkle on her shoulder.

"It will be a great *experiment*," she said, starting down the road.

Epilogue:
Once, in Baveria

Once, at the bottom of a valley in Baveria, stood a tiny tavern selling beds by the night, beer by the glass, and garlic sausages by the plateful. Through the valley ran a wind so fast it could carry the hairs from your head and the fingers from your hands. There were nights sometimes when the cold was so still and deep that it swallowed the tavern up the way a well can swallow a dropped stone. It was on a night such as this they arrived.

The young boy who owned the tavern was called Yann, and he was clearing away the supper plates when a family came in through the door. There were four of them: a man with red hair and a bow tie; a woman with goggles over her eyes, a scarf over her mouth, and a woolly hat over her head; a fat gray pigeon; and a girl with wide, wonderful eyes.

The whole tavern went silent.

Then the girl spoke. "I've something magic to give you all."

"What is it?" asked Yann.

"It's called snow," said the girl.

"What is snow?"

"It'll fall soon, and you'll see," she said. "It falls as we arrive and vanishes as we leave."

"But what does snow do?"

The girl with wonderful eyes smiled at that question, as if it had been asked many times before.

"It makes winter beautiful," she said.

Everyone around the tavern muttered and stared. Yann bit his lip. To be able to turn this cold, gray winter into something beautiful was magic indeed. But how much did this magic cost? As if sensing his question, the girl spoke: "All I ask for in return are two beds to sleep in, breakfast in the morning, and a little dish of carrot peel for my pigeon."

Yann looked at each of the villagers, wondering if they wanted to say yes as much as he did.

They consented with grave nods, so he smiled at the strangers and shook their hands (and wing), each in turn.

"Thank you," said the girl. "We'll sign the ledger."

"Wait just a minute," said Yann. "Where is this snow, then?"

The girl smiled, raising her finger, and pointed to the window.

Yann and the villagers crowded around the glass. They wiped the condensation away and all of them— every single one—let out a gasp. Outside, the snow was falling, and it was white and silent as the angels.

Yann had never been so speechless. He and the villagers stared out the window. Looking at the snow. Looking at the snow. Then he said to the girl, "But what is your name?"

Yann turned away from the window, but she and her family had already crept discreetly away to their beds. So he rushed to the ledger and looked at what the girl had written, in blue ink.

She hadn't signed her name at all.

It just said, *Snow Merchant.*

Acknowledgments

I am extremely grateful to the following alchemists, who poured so many wonderful ingredients into the pages of this book:

Julia Green, Steve Voake, and the writers at Bath Spa University added reams of comments, tons of suggestions, and packet after packet of biscuits. Then Janine Amos gave it all a good stir. My agent Becky Bagnell kept things bubbling away. Finally, Eloise King and Charlie Sheppard at Andersen Press pulled it out of the cauldron when it was ready. And Mum, as ever, sorted out the mess I made.

Thank you all.